Lock Down Publications and Ca$h
Presents

I0680391

Thug of Spades
Blood in my Tears

Written By
Corey Robinson

Copyright © 2023 Corey Robinson
Thug of Spades

All rights reserved. No part of this book may be reproduced in any
form or by electronic or mechanical means, including information
storage and retrieval systems without permission in writing from the
publisher, except by a reviewer who may quote brief passages in
review.

First Edition 2023

Printed in the United States of America

This is a work of fiction. Names, characters, places, and incidents either
are products of the author's imagination or are used fictitiously. Any
similarity to actual events or locales or persons, living or dead, is
entirely coincidental.

Lock Down Publications
P.O. Box 944
Stockbridge, GA 30281
www.lockdownpublications.com

Like our page on Facebook: Lock Down Publications
www.facebook.com/lockdownpublications.ldp

Stay Connected with Us!

Text **LOCKDOWN** to 22828 to stay up-to-date with new releases, sneak peaks, contests and more…

Like our page on Facebook:
Lock Down Publications

Join Lock Down Publications/The New Era Reading Group

Visit our website:
www.lockdownpublications.com

Follow us on Instagram:
Lock Down Publications

Email Us: We want to hear from you!

Acknowledgements

Ca$h... The best to ever do it. Thank you for believing in me and for giving me the opportunity to make my dreams come true. I know with you as my guide, I'll flourish and only get better.

Mom... I'm finally living my dream as an author, and I hope that I've made you proud. I miss you and love you. May you rest in peace.

My sisters & brothers... Marie, Julie, Jeff and Early you traveled this road with me and never veered. Thank you from the bottom of my heart for never giving up on me. I love y'all.

To the Ladies of Lowell... Always remember, the only person that can stop you from fulfilling your dreams is you. So go for what you know and never give up.

To D.G... Thanks for taking the time out and bringing new meaning to my life. I truly cherish everything and appreciate you never turning Carrie on me.

Dedicated to the Loving Memory of...
Anthony "Amp" Gray
11/1/73 – 1/25/18
May you Rest In Peace!!

PROLOGUE

"Girl, that nigga knows he is fine. I'm gonna pull his ass and get me some of that." Kiara said to her best friend Kayla while she licked her lips and stared at the man lustfully.

"Ugh! What the hell are you gonna do with his old ass Kiara? That dick has probably done been around the block a few times. He's probably full of them worms that old people get. Besides, when he finds out how old you are he aint gonna fuck with you."

Kiara rolled her eyes, sucked her teeth, and said. "Fuck you Kayla. He aint that damn old and you already know that I am not telling him I'm only fifteen. Shit, fifteen-year-olds don't' walk around with this much ass. I know I can pass for at least nineteen. Just watch ya girl work. You never know. You might just learn something."

Kayla shook her head and watched her best friend sashay over to the Boss of the streets. Twenty-four-year-old Daymion Myers had came a long way. All the status and the treasures he had obtained was well deserved. He wasn't your average drug dealer with tight pockets. Daymion shared his wealth with those who needed it most. There was hardly ever anyone that he turned away. He wasn't really fond of violence but there had been a couple of times where he'd had no choice but to use it. Most of the block respected Daymion's gangster but even then, there would still be haters.

He had been introduced to the dope game when he was around fourteen years old. His older brother Trey schooled him on all the ins and outs of the streets and even gave him his own stash house. Daymion had been taught how to handle his own customers and even counted his own money. Trey gave him his own gun when he turned sixteen and taught him how to use it. He could hit a target just as well as any veteran in the game. He had been brave for his age and handled his shit like a pro in the ring.

Daymion had idolized his brother over all other things so when Trey's life was cut short by a crack fiend in a robbery attempt, his life had been changed forever. When it first happened he wanted to seek revenge but he remembered what Trey had always told him, "This the life I chose lil Bro. You only in it because of me and that shit wasn't fair to you, so make better choices. There are consequences to this life and if something ever happens to me, don't go around here wit'cha guns blazin. Keep living and that way I can keep living through you. Be more to your people that I ever was!"

Chapter 1

Sixteen Years Later
KIARA

The sounds of moaning had awakened young Dre from his slumber. It was something he had fought hard to obtain due to the hunger pangs that rumbled in his stomach. He sat up and reached over to the box that sat beside his bed as a makeshift nightstand. The small clock radio that occupied it wasn't that great, but it still told the time and that one FM station still held some tunes.

The bright red digits on the clock revealed that it was almost three o'clock in the morning. Way too early for Dre's mind to function properly so he laid back down while a country song he had never heard played in the darkness of the morning. However, the music didn't block out the words his mother shouted from the next room.

"Yes daddy, beat this pussy up. This yo' shit."

Kiara brought in a different man almost every night when she came in from work at the strip club. Kiara told Dre that those different men is what kept a roof over their heads and food on their table, but he just didn't understand why she couldn't choose one and leave it at that. He wished that there was something he could do to help his mother, but he was not sure if anyone would give him a job. No one would hire an inexperienced youth from the hood so he would just have to wait a few more years.

Maybe get some type of training under his belt and then find something suitable. No matter how hard he tried, Dre could not go back to sleep. He thought about the man that his mother said was his father. A man he had never met and had also never heard his mother say anything good about. Kiara told Dre that Daymion Myers had forced her to have sexual relations with him when she was only fifteen. When she became pregnant, her parents forced her to press statutory rape charges against him. She said that it was hard to prove at first but when Dre was born, a DNA test was done. Kiara promised Daymion that if he signed the birth certificate and married her, she would drop the charges. Daymion agreed to sign on the line as Dreighton's father but refused to have anything else to do with Kiara. He was now sitting in a prison cell doing a mandatory twenty years. He didn't believe she would really send the crackas to his door but when she did, he had a small amount of drugs on him.

Dre felt the hunger pangs as they entered his stomach again, but he decided that instead of fighting it and going back to sleep, he would get up and go try to find something to eat. Kiara's moans got louder when he walked out of his room. Dre shook his head and walked to the bathroom so he could relieve himself of his early morning piss. When he was done, he washed his hands with the small piece of dust covered soap that sat on the edge of the sink and then proceeded to the kitchen. When he passed his mother's room, the door was slightly ajar, and he couldn't help but to peek inside. It had been open halfway, a bad habit his mother had, and that night was no different. Dre's eyes grew big as he watched the fat white man pound into his mother from behind. She must have felt his presence because she looked up and hollered, "Get your little ugly ass away from my door. Don't you see I'm busy?"

Dre turned and practically ran into the wall. His mother's blatant disrespect had gotten old, she never held any regard to what it did to his mental. When he got to the kitchen, he opened the refrigerator door. The shelves were sparse, but he managed to find a gallon milk jug with just enough left in it for a bowl of cereal. He shut the door and sat the milk on the table and then pulled a chair up to the cabinet so he could reach it. In it, he found a box of his favorite cereal, Lucky Charms. He found a bowl in the sink full of dirty dishes and ran some water in it to rinse it out. He then pulled the drawer out and found a spoon to eat the only meal he had. His stomach growled even louder when he opened up the cereal box and poured the cereal into his bowl. He licked his lips in anticipation of his first bite but when he dipped the spoon in and shoveled the cereal onto the spoon's wedge, a small roach crawled out and ruined everything.

Dre was so disappointed and so hungry he wanted to cry. There was no way he'd be able to go back to bed without putting something in his empty stomach. He couldn't bother his mother because he knew she would curse his ass out if he fucked up her money. There was only one place he knew he could escape to, and they never got mad when he showed up.

***

Kayla thought she was dreaming when she heard the knock at her door but the persistence made her realize that it was real. She opened her eyes slowly and looked at the clock. "Who the hell is at my door this early?" She asked out loud and then got out her warm cozy bed to answer it.

"Whoever the hell is out here is about to get cursed the fuck out," she said to herself as she undid the locks. When she flung the door open and saw Dre, her heart completely melted.

"Dre, what the hell are you doing out here this time of morning?" she put a hand on his shoulder and guided him inside.

Dre looked at her and said innocently, "My momma got some fat white man over there and I couldn't sleep."

Kayla loved Dre as if he were her own son. She had tried on several attempts to become pregnant, but it had just not been in her cards. She felt bad for Dre because she knew deep down that Kiara hated him. She had only kept him in hopes of making Daymion want to be with her, but her plans fell through. Daymion had felt deceived because Kiara told him that she was nineteen when they met. Daymion was no pedophile so when he found out she was only fifteen, he immediately ended things not knowing he had already planted a seed.

Kayla heard Dre's stomach growl and it caused her heart to skip a beat. "Are you hungry, my Spade?" She had called him Spade for years because she wanted him to know how great he really was. She had told him an ace of spades was considered the strongest and highest card in the deck, even above all other aces. It held the power to eliminate even the best hands. She wanted him to believe that no matter what he had been through, he would always come out on top.

"Yeah, Auntie Kay. I tried to eat some cereal, but the roaches beat me to it."

The two shared a laugh and hug and then she led him to the kitchen where she planned on making him a nice, hot breakfast. She ended up cooking enough for a small army because she wanted to make sure he had plenty to eat. She sat down at the table with him and after he took his first bite, he asked her something she had been waiting on him to ask for years.

"Auntie Kay. Can you take me to meet my dad?"

Kayla, although elated, almost choked on her food at the sound of his words. She wasn't exactly sure what to say but she was aware of the fact that Kiara had painted an ugly picture of Daymion Myers. She thought about her friend and didn't want to betray her, but someone had to step up and give a fuck about the boy that sat in front of her. Kayla took a second and swallowed her food and then answered, "Yeah, Dreighton. I will take you to meet your dad."

"Is everything my momma said about him true?"

She put her fork down on her plate and looked him in the eyes. "How about you ask him yourself?"

***

"Myers, you got a visitor," the burly looking guard yelled out in the wing that Daymion lived on.

He had been embedded in a game of spades and wasn't expecting a visitor, so he ignored the guard.

A couple of minutes later, the guard yelled out his name again. "Myers, you got a visitor. Get your ass in gear."

Daymion finally got up from the table but not before he talked a little shit. "Ya'll bitches just got saved because I had a killer hand and was about to spank that ass."

His spades partner laughed while their opponent threw their cards on the table and talked shit back.

"Nah, mane, that ass was about to get tapped. That visit is saving your pussy ass."

"Yeah, mufucka, hurry up and get back so we can finish giving you this ass whooping."

Daymion held mad respect behind the walls that he had spent almost seventeen years in. It had been a tough pill to swallow but there was nothing he could have done about it. If only he would have kept his dick in his pants, he would still have been a free man. He thought about Kiara from time to time but not because he gave a fuck about her. It was only because she had his son. He woke up every day and thought about the things he wanted to do with his seed once he returned to the streets. He couldn't wait to get to know him and could only hope that Dre felt the same way. He was certain that Kiara had tainted his image and knew that anything she had told his son couldn't have been good.

Daymion was searched and led into the visitation room where he stood for a minute and looked around. Over the years, random women had come to visit him, trying to cuff the hustler, but he wasn't focused on a relationship. Over time the visits stopped, and he felt like the women finally understood the reality of his situation. When he didn't recognize anybody in the room, he turned around to walk back out. "Man, this here is some bullshit." He turned and looked back at the slew of visitors one last time and when he did, his eyes locked on something familiar. "It can't be!" He slowly and carefully walked over to the table where the young boy with the eyes and a face like his sat.

The boy looked up at him but said nothing. All Daymion could do was stare at the presence before him as his eyes began to water.

The sound of the female voice broke the silent interchange between the two. "Hello, Daymion. I'm Kayla. Um, I'm so sorry that we just popped up like this, but Dreighton asked to meet you."

Daymion remembered Kayla from all the times she had hung out with Kiara but the woman in front of him wasn't that same young girl. Kayla had grown into her womanhood perfectly and it almost made him forget that he was in a prison visitation room. Her voice broke him from his trance once again, "Um, Daymion. I hope you're not upset about this. He just. He wanted to meet his father and I knew that Kiara would never bring him."

"No. No. No. I'm. I-I just don't know what to say. Oh my God. I've waited for this moment every day since they had me sign the birth certificate. My God, you look just like me."

Dreighton looked up to the man that had created him and then stood up. He walked around the table to where Daymion stood and when he stopped in front of him, Daymion looked him in the eyes. As soon as he did Dreighton wrapped his arms around his neck and cried like a newborn that had just entered the world.

Kayla's heart broke because no matter what Kiara had said about Daymion, Dreighton still held love for him. Kayla had asked Kiara so many times why she hated Daymion so much when he had done nothing wrong, and she always had the same response. "Fuck that nigga. That bastard could have married me, and we could have lived happily ever after. But nah, his bitch ass wanted to kick me to the curb like I wasn't good enough to be wifey. Fuck him. He can make one of them niggas in there his bitch now and as long as I got air in my lungs, he will never be around my son."

After Dreighton and Daymion let each other go from their long embrace, Kayla decided to give the two of them a moment alone, so she excused herself. "I'm gonna go get some snacks while you two catch up. Y'all got a lot of things to talk about."

"Thanks, Kayla. You can't even imagine how much this shit means to me. I owe you big time for this," Daymion said before she walked away.

As soon as they were seated, Dreighton looked at his father and asked, "Why you never wanted to meet me, Dad? My momma said you wanted to be left alone. I didn't understand."

Day looked into his son's saddened eyes and as hard as he tried not to talk down on Dre's mother, he had to tell him the truth. He didn't want the start of their relationship to be built on lies and misunderstandings. Dre deserved to know how everything went down and why he had not been in his life.

"Son, I've tried all your life to be in your life, but your mother wouldn't allow it. If I would have been out in them streets, nothing could have kept me from you." He paused long enough to wipe away the lone tear that had fallen from his eye and then continued. "Look Dre, I don't know what all your mother has told you about me but don't believe any of it. I was good to her, but she lied to me about her age. I had to step away. By the time I found out the truth, you had already been created and you are the best thing that came of that relationship."

"So, why did you leave me and not come back for me? Why did you leave me with her? She hates me. My momma hates me," Dre said as the tears flowed from his eyes and made trails down his cheeks.

Daymion responded once again with the truth. "Your mom tried to force me to marry her, but she was only a child herself. I agreed to sign the papers as your father, but I refused to be tied down to a woman I didn't want after she had lied to me about her age. I just couldn't trust her anymore. When I stopped fucking with her, she retaliated and sent them crackas to my front door. Bitch knew I had dope on me but I also had a gun, and that sealed the deal. But I've thought about you every day."

"So, when you coming home, pops? I don't wanna go back there."

Daymion could see fear in Dre's eyes and wondered why he didn't want to go back to Kiara's. He asked, "Yo son, what's up with your mom? Why you don't want to go back to her?"

Before Dre could answer, Kayla walked back up to the table, and even though Dre knew Kayla cared about him, he didn't want to trash his mother in front of her. He wasn't too sure if Kayla would go back and repeat what he said so he held onto his words. Thankfully, Daymion didn't press him for an answer.

The three enjoyed their snacks and enjoyed the time they had but soon, the guard came around and hollered. "Visitation is over. All inmates need to rise and gather on the right side of the visitation room. All visitors need to remain seated until all inmates have left the room."

He embraced his son once again and reassured him, "Don't ever think that I don't love you son. I'll be home soon and when I get there, I'm gonna make up for every second we have missed. I give you my word." He then turned to Kayla and said, "You can't even imagine how much this meant to me. Thank you." He turned to walk away but turned back around, "Yo Kayla, don't make this the last time I see you." Kayla smiled and nodded before Daymion walked out with the other inmates.

The ride back was eerily quiet but she knew that Dre was lost in his own thoughts, so she let him be. All that changed when she pulled up to the apartment complex that they lived in. "Bitch where the hell have you been with my son?" Kiara hollered as she yanked the passenger side door open. She grabbed Dreighton's arm and yanked him out of the car. She then screamed at him. "Get your sorry ass inside. I'll deal with you when I get done with this bitch." She then went to the front of the car where Kayla stood and got in her face. "Bitch don't you ever take my son anywhere without checking with me first. You are not his mother." She walked off and left Kayla standing there shaking her head.

Kayla knew that Kiara had issues, but she didn't have to talk to her and Dre that way. She knew that there was nothing she could do so she went inside and slammed the door behind her. She got undressed and hopped in the shower and when the water hit her milky flesh, Daymion came to mind. He had seemed to ignite something inside of her. Kayla knew that if she entertained anything to do with Daymion all hell would break loose but somehow, she felt that it would all be worth it.

It had been a long time since she'd been touched, and her nipples hardened at the sound of his name. "Oh Daymion." She liked how it sounded coming off of her lips and hoped that one day she could say it while he was deep inside of her. Kayla lifted a leg and propped it up on the wall and made herself feel the pleasure that she wished Daymion Myers was giving her.

***

"Damn, nigga, you look like you just came from a visit with some pussy," Branch stated when Daymion stepped back into their cell. Day and Branch had been cellmates for over three years and had become like brothers. Their release dates were only months apart with Branch going home first. Daymion believed him when he said he'd have everything set up for him as soon as he bounced, which was only a couple of months away.

Daymion was still a little emotional from his visit, but he managed to tell Branch about his son and the woman who brought him. "B, man I ain't never been attracted to a white girl or should I say woman but damn. Man, Kayla opened up something inside of me." He paused to gather his words and then said with a smile, "Man, she brought Dre to meet me. I met my fuckin seed, dawg. I finally met him and that lil muthafucka looks just like me."

Branch held his hand up, high fived Daymion and said, "Damn Day. I'm happy for you. That's all you've talked about all the years I been your bunkie and that shit finally happened. What about his momma? What's going on with her?"

Daymion cut evil eyes up at Branch and said, "I'm gon' end up having to kill that bitch 'bout my boy. He didn't tell me everything, but I can feel it in my gut that the bitch ain't done right by him. Ain't shit I can do, though. At least not until I bounce."

"Yo man, it's almost over. You can handle that shit soon and I'll be there to have your back," Branch said in a sincere voice.

Daymion nodded. "Yeah, man thanks. I just hope I can save him in time."

That night while Daymion laid in bed, he couldn't get Dre and Kayla off his mind. He thought about all the places he would take Dre and all the things he would teach him. His son was still young, and Daymion could only hope that he made it home before Dre became a product of his environment.

When the thoughts switched to the things he wanted to share with Kayla, his dick hardened. "Lay down, Lucky," he said to his dick. He had named his dick Lucky because he had pushed it up in some good pussy. Pussy that other motherfuckers could only dream of pushing up in, but he had never pushed up in some white pussy and he couldn't wait to see if it tasted different than any other dish he had tried. Daymion loved his black queens but he was just ready for a change in his life, and he thought that maybe Kayla would be a good one.

His thoughts suddenly shifted to Kiara and anger consumed him. "You fuckin' bitch. I don't know what you out there doing to my boy but you gon' pay for that shit when I get outta here." He thought about that look of fear Dre had in his eyes before Kayla walked up and interrupted them. He hoped that Kayla would bring Dre to see him again because if she did, he was going to make damn sure he found out the truth. That way, he could plan exactly how he would handle it.

Chapter 2

Dre had just fallen asleep when Kiara busted into his room and disturbed his peace. "Where in the hell did that bitch take you and you better not lie."

Dre's thoughts had been so consumed with his father that it had made it hard for him to fall asleep. It was as if his mother had intentionally waited for him to get comfortable before she barged in and as always, ruined everything. He lied there as if he didn't hear her but she was adamant and wasn't leaving his room until she had an answer.

Kiara pulled off the tattered blanket that covered him and asked again. "Where did she take you Dre? Huh? Answer the damn question."

Dre refused to snitch out Kayla so he made up a quick lie. "She took me out to breakfast and then the arcade so I could play some video games with the other guys. That's all." He felt bad about lying to her but what other choice did he have? If she found out that he had went and met his dad she'd be even more pissed.

"Oh yeah, you wanna go play video games with some other guys? How about you go out on them corners and play games with those niggas that's gonna put some money in your pocket?"

"Ma please, I'm tired. I haven't been getting much sleep at night. Please just let me be. I promise I'll go out and find me some kind of work but right now I just wanna sleep ma."

Kiara wasn't trying to hear what he was saying so she grabbed his arm and pulled him up. She bent over to where they were face to face and as the spittle flew from her mouth. She told him how she really felt. "You listen to me and you listen good. If your ass wants to eat and keep laying up in here at night, then I suggest you take your ass out there and put in some work. You're old enough to take care of yourself and to help me out with other things around here. I'm done taking care of you." She pushed him back on the bed and walked out slamming the door behind her.

The tears threatened his eyes but he refused to cry. His father would kill Kiara if he knew what was really going on but still he wished that he would have told him everything.

He finally got up from his sleep deprived stupor and got dressed in some jeans that hung off his ass like a real street thug. He pulled the cleanest shirt he could find over his head and went into the bathroom so he could wash his face and brush his teeth. He was tired of his mothers' bullshit so when he looked up at his reflection in the mirror he stated. "I'm about to go out here and get paid and when I get enough money, I'm getting' outta this bitch."

He went back to his room and slid on the only pair of shoes he had that fit his growing feet. After he laced them up, he walked out of his room. When he walked past his mother's door, he noticed her sitting on the floor beside her bed with a clear glass pipe in her hand. She must have felt his presence because she stopped what she was doing and looked up into his eyes.

"What the hell are you looking at?"

He didn't even waste his breath to answer her. Instead, he shook his head and walked away. It was time for him to grow up and he knew just what he was going to do get himself started.

***

Dory nursed the blunt he had filled with the Kush while he sat on the steps outside of the trap house. He took a long, slow pull and looked up just in time to notice the dude that walked in his direction. He had never seen him around that part of the hood before, so he didn't know what to make of his presence. He carefully and discreetly reached in his waist band and pulled his gun just in case it had been a set up. When the jit got close enough to really look at him, Dory saw something familiar in his eyes.

"Sup, lil man?" I ain't never seen you around here before. The fuck is you doing in this area?'

His gun stayed handy just to be safe. A lot of the niggas on the block got lit up from not being cautious but Dory refused to get caught slippin', like that. To him, anyone could be a threat in the streets no matter how young they were.

"I'm looking for some work. You think you could help me out?"

Dory laughed at his question and replied, "Lil nigga, you don't even know me and you stepping to me like I'm just gonna give you a fucking handout. The fuck is wrong with you."

"Come on man, I'm just trying to eat like everybody else."

"Yo, your ass look real familiar. Who is your daddy?"

"Day my daddy. What that got to do with me working?" Dre was getting agitated with the man. Either he was going to give him what he asked for or not.

Dory was shocked at the info the kid had told him. He remembered the opportunity that Daymion had given him many years ago when he had approached him the same way that he did. He wondered how Daymion would feel about him putting his shadow on a corner but since Daymion Myers wasn't in a position to have an opinion, he would put him to work and use him for as long as he could. He'd take care of the rest when the time came.

"Your momma Kiara Taylor?" He licked his lips and thought about the way that Kiara had sucked his dick. He knew that she'd had a son by Daymion but he never would have guessed the he'd have the opportunity that had presented itself right then.

"What my momma got to do with anything? I ont need her permission to make some money. So, you gonna put me on or not? I can always find someone else."

"Aiight, Shawty, you wanna put in some work? Follow me."

Dory liked Dre's tough attitude and hoped that he would apply it the same way when it came to his money. Dre walked into the house behind his new boss and his heart felt like it was about to beat out of his chest. All of what he was about to do was all new to him and even though he was nervous, he was a Myers and it was what he was born for. He had hustler blood running through his veins and it was time for him to represent.

There were four other dudes in the house along with them and Dory took him around the room and introduced him to each one.

"You 'bout to meet the niggas you answer to when you can't get to me. Those two there are Big Gun and Mellow. You ever cross me, you'll find out real quick why they call him Big Gun, and Mellow is just like his name represents. Mellow as fuck but don't let that shit fool you. He'll turn up and bust a cap in that ass if you turn foul."

The two men nodded at Dre and then went back to playing their video game. Dre nodded back and was about to say something, but they were so engrossed in what they were doing that he decided to hold his words.

"Teddy, this lil nigga here is about to join the set so get to know him real good."

Teddy looked to be around three hundred pounds, but he was solid with it. He was sitting at the kitchen table with a plate full of food in front of him. He swallowed his food and acknowledged the kid in front of him.

"Sup? What they call you?"

Dre thought for a minute and decided that the name Kayla gave him would be appropriate for his mission because he planned to ride above his circumstances.

"My name is Dre, but the streets call me Spade."

Teddy could see the passion in the kids eyes and he liked that. It reminded him of his teenage years when he was hungry, and someone put him at the table so he could eat too. "Okay, so you wanna be a thug and be on the set with some real mufackas? Your ass betta not be on no bullshit cause if you are, you gon have to answer to me. You got a problem with that?"

"Nah, I ain't got no problem with that."

"That's what the fuck I thought."

Teddy picked the sandwich he had been eating back up. Dory laughed and shook his head.

"Come on Dre, that nigga just don't like to be fucked with when he got food in his hand. If he made as much money as had did meals I could've retired from the game by now."

Dory took him to meet the last member of his squad. Trap Town sat in the recliner with his head leaned back and moaned while the female in front of him sucked on the head of his dick. Dory noticed that the sex act didn't faze Dre, but he didn't know that Dre had seen his momma do it, so it was something he had been used to.

Trap Town must have felt their presence because he opened his eyes and asked, "You eva had yo dick sucked by a bad bitch like this?"

Trap Town was the most ratchet of all Dory's men. He didn't give a fuck who he disrespected or whose bitch he fucked. Nobody in their right mind tried him because they knew that he was a loose wire.

Dory looked at Dre and before he could speak, a female voice called out his name. "Dorian, baby I gotta run over to my grandfathers and take him to the doctor but I'll be back in time to make you something for dinner." She kissed Dory on the lips and then turned to look at Dre and said, "Hey cutie, I'm Shay. The real head of this house. What they call you?"

Dre looked at the female in front of him and smiled. He felt something inside of him shift. "My name is Dre."

"Well Dre, it's nice to meet you. Don't you let these niggas in here corrupt your brain, okay. I gotta go but I'll talk to you some other time."

He smiled at the beauty but when Shay left the room, Dory spoke up and said, "Don't worry lil nigga. You'll get you one like that soon but don't get no ideas about that one. That's my pussy and I'll cut that bitch throat before I let another nigga get close. You know what I'm saying?"

Dre understood the threat from Dory but pussy was the farthest thing from his mind. Dre only wanted to make some money so he could help his momma out. He had grown tired of all the men coming in and out of her bedroom so he would do what he had to do to stop it, and who knows, maybe she would even begin to treat him like somebody. If it didn't work out that way, he'd keep a nice stash until he had enough to make it on his own. But he was ready to start filling the pocket of his jeans.

Dre asked Dory, "So when you gon' give me something to start with?"

Dory rubbed the top of Dre's nappy head and said, "That's what I'm talkin' 'bout. A nigga ready to make that bread. Come on, let me show you what to do." Dre followed Dory out the back door and down a trail that went through the woods. When they came out on the other side, he took him to another house. Dory noticed that Dre looked confused. "Rule number one, never shit where you sleep. Keep it close to get to but far enough away not get caught with it. You gon be a natural but don't get too cocky when those ends start stacking. You gonna always be the worker and I'ma always be the boss. You remember that and we won't have no problems."

Dory could tell that Dre still didn't understand so he said, "Don't worry kid, you'll understand soon enough."

***

Kayla sat and thought about Daymion with a smile on her face. She had been attracted to him all those years ago but unlike Kiara she knew that she was too young to pursue him. Plus, she didn't wanna have to fight her best friend.

Kayla had grown up in the hood right down the street from Kiara. They met in kindergarten and had been friends since. Kayla had also always liked black men. The smooth color of their skin and the pep in their step made her juices flow but she didn't have any luck in the relationship department. She told herself that she was swearing off men until she found the right one and had managed to stick to that for the last couple of years. Daymion Myers could be the one to make her change her mind. She decided that she would get up early Saturday morning and go see him again. She just had to see if he felt the same connection to her as she did to him.

The sudden banging on the door broke her from her thoughts and caused her to jump. "Damn who the hell is at my door?" As soon as she opened it, she regretted it immediately.

"Bitch, where the fuck is my son?" Kiara asked as she walked through the door. Kiara began to walk through

Kayla's apartment as she looked for Dre, but she was looking in the wrong place.

Kayla slammed her front door and said to Kiara, "I haven't seen him since you snatched him outta my car. Maybe if you weren't so busy with all those men you could keep better tabs on him."

Kiara turned and ran up on Kayla but missed when she swung at her. "Look bitch, I do what I gotta do so I can take care of my son. I have to do it all by my damn self so don't fuckin judge me. His sorry ass daddy should've made sure my son didn't do without but his ass couldn't handle the pressure."

Kayla got up in Kiara's face, "Judge you. Bitch, you ain't worth the time and it's your own damn fault that Daymion is not here to take care of him. You put him where he's at so don't talk shit about it now."

Kiara looked at Kayla funny., "You takin' up for that nigga? You got some damn nerve. You supposed to be my friend but you takin up for the enemy. That's flaw as fuck."

"Daymion is not your enemy, Kiara. You lied to him, not the other way around so stop blaming him for not being here. He didn't choose to be put behind bars for all these years. You chose that for him because he didn't want to be with you," Kayla then opened her front door back up as she said, "Get outta here and don't ever fuckin' knock on my door again. You don't deserve Daymion Myers or the son he gave you, and you don't deserve my friendship."

"Fine, but I better not ever see my son over here again or I'm a put your ass where Daymion is," Kiara said and then walked out with Kayla slamming the door behind her.

***

Dre was the new kid on the block so his first night didn't go as he had hoped, but he was able to make a few dollars. He felt like no one would take him seriously, but he would surely change their minds. He kept the package stashed under his nut sack, a spot he had seen one of his mother's tricks store it one night when they were getting dressed.

Two boys that looked to be around his age tried to run up on him but Dre kept a poker face the entire time. He stood his ground until one of the men pulled out a weapon. He wasn't ready to die over some bullshit that early in the game. "We know you out here with something muthafucka so just go ahead and give that shit up" The two boys ended up taking the Timbs off of his feet, but Dre made sure to etch their faces to his memory because once he got to a level up, he would make them pay for what they'd done.

After the incident happened, he decided to call it a night, so he took off down the block. He barely made it to the next block when a black Mazda 929 pulled up beside him. The dark tint of the windows concealed the driver's identity and he hoped that it wasn't a hit or even some undercovers. The windows slowly rolled down and when he saw who was behind it, he breathed a sigh of relief. Shay looked at him and smiled and with raised brows, looked down at his feet.

"What happened to your shoes, Spade?"

He gave her a funny look and pressed his lips together. "Call me Dre. Spade is only for them niggas who need to understand I'm 'bout to change the rules to the game."

"Okay, Okay. I hear you straightening me on your name but that still doesn't explain where your shoes are at."

"I gave them to someone who needed them worse than me. Why you called me Spade anyway? I ain't neva told you that so how did you know?"

"I heard you tell Teddy that earlier. He's my big brother. You gotta excuse him though, he only plays hard with people he's drawn to. He must have seen something in you he liked.

He's harmless as long as you don't come between him and his dinner. Come on, you want a ride?"

"Yeah, but I need to go check in with Dory first."

"That's fine. I was headed back there anyway."

Dre was quiet for a second because he wanted to choose his next words wisely. He cut his eyes over to Shay and took in her beauty. He had never seen a female so perfect, his Auntie Kayla came close, but Shay broke the mold. She felt his stare and smiled.

"Something you wanna say to me? You looking like you want to speak."

"I'm sorry, I'm just trying to figure out what you doing with Dory? You seem a little young to be with him!"

"Really? Well, I'm eighteen and I have my reasons for being with him. He can be a good guy sometimes. Why you so concerned?"

"No reason, just trying to figure shit out. He's already warned me so you ain't gonna have to worry about me."

"Well, that's a little disappointing because I wouldn't have minded worrying a little."

She smiled as she drove off and headed to the house where Dory would be waiting.

Chapter 3

Daymion stared at the photo he had pulled from the envelope he'd received at mail call. The photo was of Dre but he felt like he was looking in the mirror. He was in awe of how much Dre looked like him. It was as if Daymion had made him all by himself without any help from Kiara. The time he had spent in prison would be all worth it once he was released. He couldn't wait to get on the court and shoot some hoops with his son. He hoped that Dre would be interested in those type of things. Daymion swore that he would be the father he needed when he was growing up.

"Yo Day, what's up bruh? You look like you in another world and shit. What's that you looking at?"

Daymion looked up at Branch and smiled proudly and showed the photo to his cellmate and friend.

"That's him B. That's my boy. I made that lil nigga right there. That's all me. "

The two friends shared a laugh right before Daymion pulled another photo from the envelope. "Yo Kayla sent me that flick of him but she also sent me this one. Check it out."

"Dayum, Day. White girl pretty as fuck. She might be somebody you can actually start a life with. I mean, I know you said you was feeling her when she brought your seed but lil momma could be the one. She look like she got her shit together."

"Yeah, B she may be just what I need in my life. I ain't trying to go back out there like I was. I plan on keepin' it low pro this time around an it would be real nice to have someone by my side to share it all with. I need a bitch that's gonna stand beside me not one that will bring me down."

"Yeah bruh, I know just what you mean by that. Good women are hard to find so you better hold on to that one."

The room grew quiet as both men laid back and drowned themselves in their own thoughts. Time passed slow while their minds raced. Daymion was the first to break the silence between them.

"Shawty put a letter in the envelope with those flicks. She sent me her number, wants me to call and she wants to come see me this weekend."

Branch was happy for his friend because he had always felt like Daymion got fucked over. He didn't know him back then but he knew exactly what some pussy would make a man do. In a male prison pedophile are a disgrace and often get jumped on but everyone knew the position that Kiara had put Daymion in and they were well aware of the fact that it could have happened to them too. So, everyone held respect for him from day one.

"I'm happy for you Day, but didn't you mention that the white girl was your baby momma's best friend? How you think she gon' act knowing ya'll fuckin around."

"I'm sure her stupid ass is going to be pissed but fuck her. She done stole enough of my joy and I'll kill her ass before I let her take anymore."

"Oh yeah? Well, that might be just what you have to do."

***

The apartment was strangely quiet when Dre walked in and he breathed a sigh of relief. He had expected his momma to be there waiting to curse his ass out but he figured she was probably out with some random nigga. He walked past her room on the way to his and peeked inside just to make sure he was really alone. He noticed the glass pipe sitting on her nightstand and walked in the room. He picked it up and took a look at it trying to imagine just what she got out of it. He sat it back down where he'd gotten it and reached in his pants pulling out what was left of the package he'd been given. He pulled one of the small rocks out of the baggie and sat it on the nightstand beside the pipe and walked out.

He then walked to his own room and sat on the edge of his bed and pulled out the small load of money he had made. He had given Dory his cut already so what he possessed was all his. The first thing he planned on doing was buying a new pair of shoes and maybe even a couple outfits from the Goodwill store downtown. He didn't have designer money so he would settle with what he could afford. He counted the money with pride and although, it wouldn't seem like much to a veteran dealer it was a lot to him. It was more money than his hands had ever held. Too bad, his hands wouldn't hold it for long.

"Where in the hell did you get that damn money?"

He hadn't even heard Kiara burst into his room so she caught him completely off guard. He tried to push the bills back into his pocket but she was faster than him and snatched it right from his grip.

"I went, I – I went and put in some work like you told me to but I need that money to buy me some more shoes so give it back."

"Some shoes? Where the hell are your shoes at and who gave you some work?"

Dre refused to tell her that Dory had put him on so once again he had to tell her a lie. "I ont know who they was. They was just trying to help me out. I need that money ma!. I left something for you by the pipe you be sucking on."

She counted the money she had snatched out of his hand and then pulled a bill out to give him back. "Here, I'm a give you back five dollars but I'm keeping the rest. I've been taking care of you by myself ever since I pushed you out and because of that, you owe me this. You should be glad that I'm giving you anything," she turned to walk out of his room but before she closed the door behind her, she turned to him once more, "You need to go wash your ass cause you smelling a little **musky**, and don't use my soap. You got some money now, so go buy your own."

When she slammed the door behind her he looked down at the crumpled five-dollar bill and shook his head. He wasn't a little kid anymore and he was tired of being treated like a bastard. He lifted up his right arm and smelled the aroma of sweat that came out of his pores. He was so embarrassed and hoped that Shay hadn't smelled it too. Kiara only gave him the bare necessities so he had to make do. He had been ashamed to attend school so he missed a lot of days. So many that he was kicked out when he turned sixteen. He didn't miss it though, the shit they tried to teach him had been boring so they did him a favor.

He thought of all the ways he could keep his mother at bay. He could keep her drug supply up but that would make his cuts even smaller so he bashed that idea. He could run away but he had nowhere else to go. He knew that first place Kiara would look was Kayla's so he definitely couldn't go there. His mind continued to race. There had to be something that would get his mother off his back but once he figured it out, he hoped that he would have the nerve to pull through.

***

Shay walked in and heard the conversation that Dory and his boys were having and got pissed.

"Aye, where that lil nigga come from anyway?" Big Gun inquired.

"Nigga, that's Daymion's son."

31

"You mean Daymion Myers? Ain't that mufucka locked up? How the hell he got a son?" Big Gun had never met Daymion, but his name came up in a lot of hood gossip. The streets respected the nigga and him being in prison didn't change a thing.

"Yeah, he locked up but he planted that seed before he went in. He was fucking with Kiara Taylor and got her pregnant before he found out that she was only a child herself and since he aint want her ass, she booked him. When them mufuckin crackers ran in on him he was dirty and wasn't shit he could say. Nigga got caught slippin."

Trap Town cut into the conversation, "Mane, I be seeing that bitch Kiara shaking her ass up in Kronics but they say that bitch be smoking up her tips. You sho' your shit safe with her son?"

"That lil mufucka better stash my shit when he at home where she can't get to it. Jit might be new to this but that don't make him exempt from getting a cap busted in that ass. These hollow points don't discriminate."

Shay felt bad for Dre and planned on having a talk with Dory, because she didn't agree with the things him and his crew had said. She had taken a liking to him and decided to take him under her wing from that day on. She'd make sure his money was always straight before he reported back to Dory and if it wasn't she'd give him what he needed to make it right even if it cost her in the end.

***

The old white sales lady adjusted the glasses on her face when the young black kid entered the store. She wondered if he was by himself or if he had a gang of hoodlums waiting for him outside. She had never seen him before and surely, she didn't trust him. She looked down and noticed that he didn't have on any shoes, only socks. Strange, she thought. He had to have seen the sign posted outside that read, "NO

SHIRT, NO SHOES, NO SERVICE." That would give her a valid reason to kick him out but then she decided that he probably couldn't read.

She came from behind the counter once she lost sight of him. She'd be damned if she allowed a black kid to steal from her establishment. She walked around until she found him in front of a shoe rack.

"Excuse me young man. Is there something that I could help you with?"

Dre looked into the beady eyes of the old woman. Her round, gold trimmed glasses seemed too small for her face and stopped right at the tip of her nose. She was dressed in a flower print top and a pink knee length skirt. Her crocheted sweater was tight on her slender arms and her wrinkled hands were perched on her hips while she spoke to him.

He pulled the shoe off that he had tried on and acknowledged the lady, "Nah, I'm good. Just trying to find me a decent pair of shoes that's all."

"Where are your parents? Do you have money to pay for some shoes because you are not walking out of here with anything unless you pay for it. Do you understand me?"

Dre gave her a strange look because he knew what she had implied but she had the wrong idea about him. "Yes ma'am, I got money. I wasn't gonna leave without paying for them. I ain't no thief. I know better."

"Yeah, well you better pay for them because I will call the police and have you arrested if you don't. Now hurry up and find what you need and leave my store before I kick you out of here."

The lady crossed her arms over her chest angrily and continued to stand there and watch him.

Another customer was at the counter but all she cared about was keeping an eye on Dre. She yelled out to the other patron. "I'll be with you in a moment. I got a black boy back here that I need to keep my eye on."

Dre shook his head and tried on another pair of shoes that fit perfectly on his growing feet. He looked at the lady and smiled and then turned and walked to a rack of clothes, the lady still on his ass close behind. He purposely took his time and picked out some jeans and a black t-shirt with an Ace of Spades on the front. He found a two pack of white boxers and walked to the counter so that he could pay for the purchases.

The other customer stood to the side and waited. She was ready to pay for her things but allowed Dre to go ahead of her. The sales lady cleared her throat and pointed down at Dre's feet so he took the shoes off and placed them on the counter also. He still couldn't believe that she had treated him like she did. He was in Goodwill for God's sake, not Neiman Marcus. She rang up his things and the total came to around seven dollars. Dre pulled out his money and placed it on the counter in front of him.

"Um, I'm a little short but I could bring you the rest later on. I promise I'll come back."

The lady got an attitude and pulled all the purchases off the counter, "How about I just hold this stuff and when you get enough to pay for it, you can come back and get it then."

The other customer couldn't believe the way the lady had treated Dre, and she knew he was treated like that because he was black. She couldn't stand prejudice people so she decided to stand up for the boy.

"It's alright young fella. Put your money back in your pocket. I'll take care of it for you. I can count it as my good deed for the day."

Dre looked up at her and smiled. "Thanks ma'am. I'll pay you back one day. I give you my word."

"No son, You don't owe me anything. You just keep yourself out of trouble. That will do me just fine."

The sales lady threw his purchases in a bag and put them on the counter with an attitude that was uncalled for. She gave the other customer a nasty look and turned back to Dre.

"Fine, now leave my establishment immediately."

Dre picked up the bag and walked out thankful that he still had some money in his pocket. He planned to stop at the grocery store a block from his place and buy some soap and deodorant. If he was lucky, he'd find it cheap and still be able to buy himself a bag of funyuns, his favorite. It would be his snack for when he was out on the block later. When he was done, he headed home and walked into hell.

***

"Bitch you better find my shit. I know what the fuck I had in that pack. You gonna find it or you gon have to pay for that loss."

"Come on Trell, I didn't touch your shit. I only smoked what you gave me, I swear."

"Yeah, well my shit is gone so get your ass to work and take care of it."

The man put his hand on top of Kiara's head just as he noticed a figure come into view.

"Sup kid. I was just chillin with your mom here but I aint gone be too much longer."

Kiara turned her head to see who he had been talking to and saw Dre as he stood in the doorway.

"Dammit Dre, didn't I tell your ass not to fuck with my damn money? Get your ass on somewhere and let me handle my business?"

She turned back to the man and dropped to her knees in front of him and just as she was about to unzip his jeans Dre turned and walked away. He wasn't sure how long his mother had been lost on the pipe and wished he could do something to change it. He had grown sick of niggas using her for their own guilty pleasures but until he got his level up there wasn't shit he could do about it.

Dre decided it was time to get ready for the block so he went in the small bathroom and got undressed. He turned on the shower and found the water to be freezing cold but he refused to let it stop him. He opened the three pack of Ivory soap and pulled out one bar. He put the other two behind some towels in the cabinet so his mother wouldn't find them. He rushed under the cold stream of water and chill bumps popped on his skin but after a couple of minutes his skin adjusted to the temperature and he scrubbed his body clean.

He felt so good and so refreshed when he was done and basked in the feeling before he dried off and put on some of the solid deodorant and a fresh pair of boxers. He went back to his room and found a decent pair of socks to put on because he had forgotten to buy some. Once he put on his new jeans and his Ace of Spades T-shirt and tennis shoes, he felt like a million bucks. He had intentionally gotten the jeans a size too big so they would hang off his waist like a real dope boy. He made sure his mother was still busy with her company and then snuck in her room. He opened the closet door and stood in front of the long mirror that hung on it. He admired the image that looked back at him and wondered why he hadn't started selling dope before then. He vowed that every time he made some money he would go and get a new outfit and shoes until his wardrobe was up to par.

"Now I'm ready for the block. I just hope the block is ready for me."

He looked at his reflection one last time and headed to the door. The block was waiting on him and he didn't want to be late.

Chapter 4

"Myers, lets go. Your visitor is waiting on you," the guard hollered with authority, but it was an authority he didn't need because Daymion had been ready for the visit all week.

"Aight Dawg, go on out there and lay that mack game down on snow and secure your future. I'm a be right here waiting to hear all about it when you get back." Branch gave him some dap and walked out of the room. He hoped that Kayla would bring Daymion some kind of happiness because he had been sad for so long.

Daymion walked out behind his cell mate and found him about to use the telephone. He stood and made a funny pose and asked, "So, how do I look?"

"Well, not as good as me but you still fly my nigga. You could use a better outfit but other than that, you straight."

The two men shared a laugh and then Daymion went to go see the woman who had melted his heart only a few weeks before. She hadn't mentioned bringing Dre with her but it would have been a wonderful surprise. He was anxious to get to know his son as much as he could before he bounced just in case he would be in the fight of his life once he was freed.

After being patted down, Daymion walked into the visiting room and looked right into Kayla's eyes and it comforted his soul. He was stuck on her beauty for a minute and didn't move. Once the guard noticed, he tapped him on the shoulder and broke him from his trance.

"Move it Myers, before you get sent back to your cell."

"Sorry Sir, I was just a little mesmerized."

He went to Kayla and as soon as he was in front of her, she pulled him into her arms. When she had her hands locked securely around his neck, she tiptoed and put her lips to his, but she forgot to stop and remember that Daymion hadn't felt a woman's touch in a while. His dick rose instantly and he wasn't sure if it was because they had good chemistry or if he just needed some pussy. Only time would tell.

He slowly pulled back from her and looked her up and down. "Yo, Lucky ass actin up down there so we should probably chill with all this closeness. Cause ain't shit we can do about it."

Kayla laughed and looked down to see that his dick had rocked up. She lifted her brows from the sight of his thickness and hoped that she would really be the woman he gave it to when he came home. No wonder Kiara had tried to keep a hold of him all those years ago.

"Sorry Day, but I had to get that off my chest. I've wanted to do that since I was fifteen but Kiara got to you first."

"Naw Shawty, you don't need to apologize for shit you do, you good." He licked his lips and looked her up and down once again.

They walked to the snack bar hand in hand and sat down at the table designated for them once they got what they wanted. Both ready to learn all that they could from each other.

"Oh, so you was feeling a nigga back then too? Why you ain't step to me then? Why you let that bitch Kiara get to my ass first? Shit could have turned out way different for all of us."

Kayla pursed her lips together and told him the truth." I'm sorry Daymion. I tried to talk Kiara out of stepping to you not only because I was checking you out but hell, we was only fifteen. We ain't have no business trying to mess around with a grown man. Plus, I knew the consequence you could face. I should have said something to you but I just, I didn't want to betray my best friend."

"Yeah, well how do you feel now?" Daymion needed to know just where her loyalty would lie in the end. He needed to know if her and Kiara's bond was still strong because he didn't have time for any other problems or bullshit to arise.

"You know Daymion, when Dreighton was born, he spent most of his time with me at my parents' house but when they passed away, I had to go live with my grandma. She would have shit herself if I would have brought a black man's baby into her home even if it wasn't mine. She couldn't help it, because she was raised back in those days when mixing races was shunned upon. I vowed that as soon as I turned eighteen and could get my inheritance, I'd move back. I had grown so attached to Dre and I just couldn't imagine not having him in my life."

She took a breath and continued. "Day, when I first got back in town, Dreighton wasn't looking so good. He was only a few years old and yet, Kiara hated him and she still does. You can see it in her eyes when she looks at him. She treats him like shit and because he's such a good kid, he still loves and respects her. He knocks on my door sometimes just to get away. To get a nice hot meal and a good nights sleep and she gets so pissed when she finds out. I don't know what to do. He needs you Daymion. He needs his father. Promise me that you'll save him."

Daymion's nostrils flared from anger. He couldn't believe what he'd heard. He was beyond pissed off and couldn't wait to make Kiara pay for the way she'd been treating their son. There had to be something he could do to make her treat him better. At least until he could get there.

"Hey, I got an idea that might help the situation until I can get there. Kiara only hates Dre because of me. She tried to use him as a pawn thinking it would make me be with her. If she had ever thought she didn't have a chance, I truly believe she would have gotten rid of him. If she thought we were going to be together once I get out of here, she would act totally different towards him! I think I should write her and ask her for forgiveness. Make her think we gonna be together. Maybe even get her to come see me."

"Hell no, Daymion. Why would you make her think that? She's fucking crazy and when she finds out you're playing her, there's no telling what level she'll stoop to."

Kayla pleaded with him but Daymion's mind was made up. Kiara would pay for her bullshit one way or the other and he was going to make sure of it.

***

"Uh oh, check it out. The lil nigga done cleaned up. What's up Spade?"

Teddy had to do a double take when Dre walked in. He had to admit, the kid cleaned up very well but what caught his eye was the Ace of Spade t-shirt he had on.

"Oh, shit, I see you done found a shirt that fits your personality but hold on I got something that will go perfect with that." He walked out of the room and returned with a black cap in his hands. He passed it to Dre who noticed the spade outlined in white and smiled.

"Thanks, Teddy. This right on time." "No problem kid. Go on out there and do ya thang. I'll see you later on."

"Uh, yo Teddy. One thing, can you stop calling me kid? I ain't gonna never get my respect if people hear you call me that."

"Yeah, I got it. My bad."

Dre walked away while he put on the starter cap that Teddy had given him. He was ready to get on the block and do his thang but first, he had to get his package from Dory. He knocked on the bedroom door and when it opened, Shay's pretty face stared back at him. She reminded him so much of his Auntie Kayla, only with slightly darker skin. Her long natural hair touched the middle of her back and looked as smooth as silk. She was the first female he had felt something for but he knew he had to keep his feelings in check, at least until he could make his move.

"Hey Dre, I didn't expect to see you so early and you lookin all fresh. I'm liking the look you got going on here."

Dre noticed the sheer nightgown that she had on. He could feel himself become angry and little did he know, she felt completely naked in front of him. She also felt ashamed because deep down, Dre had a hold on her. Dre thought that she was too good for Dory and too young. He hoped that one day she would realize it too.

Dory appeared butt ass naked from behind her and pulled her away from the door.

"You sho doing a lot of talking to this lil nigga. Go get your ass back in the bed. I aint done with you yet."

Dory laughed when Dre turned his head away so he wouldn't have to look at him, or his dick. "What's the matter? Act like you ain't never seen a dick before. You do have one, right?" He shook his head and laughed again and then turned around leaving the door open behind him. He climbed in the bed beside Shay and summonsed Dre in." Come on in and get that package out of that top drawer and go make me some money."

Dre did as he was told and tried not to look towards the bed but he just couldn't help himself. Seeing Shay laid up beside Dory made him wanna smash some shit up. His heart pounded with so much force, it was hard to believe that no one else heard it. He could see it in Shay's eyes how unhappy she was with Dory but she was too afraid to leave him alone.

Didn't she understand that all she had to do was give in and Dre would save her.

He got his package and headed back out the door but before he closed it behind him, he took one last look at Shay and told himself that one day he would rescue her and he meant it. Fuck the rules of the streets, he had his own agenda. He would continue to play the hand he had been given until he pulled the right card and then he would cut everyone else out. Shay would be his no matter what it cost him.

***

As soon as Daymion returned to his cell, Branch was on him, "Well, what happened? Did it go as good as you hoped it would?"

Daymion stood against the cell wall with a somber look on his face. He was happy Kayla had come to see him and enjoyed every second they shared but the things she had told him about his son had his mind and heart fucked up.

"Damn Dawg, what the hell happened out there? Shit, don't tell me she done broke your heart already."

"Nah B, it ain't even like that. Kayla is everything I could ever want and she's all a nigga deserves but she told me about the shit Kiara's been putting my son through. I'm a have to kill that bitch when I get outta here."

"Nigga you can't get out of here and start murking bitches. I mean, I know ya kid means the world to you but you ain't going to do him any good if you murder the bitch that had him you going to end up right back in here."

"At least it will be worth it."

"How Day? What you think it's gon do to that boy of yours? Huh? Losing his father all over again and possibly for the rest of his life. That boy needs some guidance. He's gon reach adult status before he's supposed to because the streets gonna suck him in and them fuckin streets don't love no damn body. My nigga, I can't let you go out like that. I got some people who could handle that for you so you don't have to get your hands dirty."

"I appreciate that gesture Bruh, but this is something I gotta handle myself. I made that mufuckin bed so I got to be the one to lie in it. I'm a give Kiara just what she's been asking for."

And he meant every word.

***

Business had been good that night for Dre. He ended up selling out of product faster than he'd ever done. He knew Dory was going to be very pleased with the news and couldn't wait to get back to the house to give him his money and re-up. He had been on the look out all night for those two boys that tried to rob him, the last time, but they had been no where in sight. He told himself that he would get a weapon so when niggas felt like they could try him he would shut them down. That was his territory now and a mufucka needed to respect it. He let out a long sigh and headed back down the trail so he could give Dory his cut.

A funny feeling came over him when he got to the house. None of Dorys' men were outside which was very unusual but maybe they had just taken a break and went in. He shrugged his shoulders and walked up on the porch. As soon as he got to the door he heard loud moaning and Dory talking shit.

"Hell yeah, This pussy good. Take this mufucka like a real bitch. Own this dick."

Dre backed away from the door because he couldn't fathom the thought of Dory treating Shay like a trick bitch. To imagine her up under the bastard made him sick but he chose not to disturb them. He would sit on the front steps and give them time to finish before he walked in. He was in no hurry to lose his innocence to a woman but when he did he hoped that it would be Shay. She was only a little over a year older than him and way more experienced but he would still give it all he had. He swore that he was the only seventeen-year-old virgin in the hood but fuck it he didn't give a fuck what people said. He wanted to share his first time with someone special.

He sat there and thought about all the things he would do to Shay once she became his but a voice he recognized spoiled his entire fantasy.

"Yeah nigga, Go head cause this your pussy tonight. Yes Dory, Yes."

Dre stood up from the steps he had sat on and walked inside to the door. He stuck his ear to it and listened just to make sure he hadn't been imagining things. When the sounds that he heard didn't deceive him, he was pissed and he decided to take a closer look.

He gripped the doorknob and slowly turned it. When the door opened he walked quietly inside and left the door open behind him. His steps were short and light as he made his way in the living room where the sounds of pleasure had come from. He stood still and watched, Dory as he stroked the women from behind. He couldn't see her face clearly because of the position she was being held in but it was as if she could feel his presence. Her eyes opened and her head turned to the side. As soon as she saw him she went off.

"What in the hell is that motherfucker doing here? Is he following me? Is this supposed to be some kind of joke?"

Dory stopped his rhythm and looked to see what had startled her. When he saw that it was Dre he kept going. "Damn woman, don't worry about his ass. Lil nigga gon have to learn one day. Might as well be now. Shit, he ain't a kid no more. Mufucka almost grown. I'm about to nut and I ain't trying to stop so ignore his ass."

Dre stood there for a minute longer and pulled out the money he had to give Dory. He walked over and threw the money down on the table in front of them. He refused to look at them again because what he had seen had disgusted him. He walked out of the living room and back out the front door. His heart couldn't have broken anymore because it had been shattered long ago but embarrassment had set in. He shut the front door behind him as Shay pulled into the driveway.

She noticed him as he stepped off the front porch and got out of her Mazda with a smile that could melt the coldest of hearts. "Hey Dre. Looks like you had a good day, whoa, or better yet a pretty crappy one." Once she got closer to him she noticed the somber look in his eyes. She put an arm around his shoulders to hopefully bring him some comfort and asked "What's going on with you? Has something happened?"

"Could you just give me a ride home?" He tried to lead her back to her ride because he didn't want Shay to witness what he already had. Not only because he felt ashamed but because he didn't want to see her hurt.

"Yeah, I could give you a ride but let me run inside real quick and say something to Dory, Okay?"

"No, um I really need to get home. Can't you talk to him when you come back?"

She looked at him strangely and wondered why he needed to get home so bad but decided not to question him. "You sure are acting funny but come on, I'll get you home. Are you sure you're okay?"

"I'm just tired and hungry. I need a little break that's all."

"Okay Dre, get in the car. I'm actually a little hungry too. Maybe we could stop and get a bite on the way. You okay with that?"

"That's cool. How about McDonalds? A nigga fucked up about they fries."

"McDonalds it is."

They both got in the vehicle and put on their seat belts. The air kicked on full blast as soon as she turned the key. Dre thought about what kind of ride he would cop when he got his paper right. He could see himself sporting a Lexus RZ45OE sitting on chromes with Shay in the seat beside him looking like the queen of the world and representing the realest nigga alive.

"What the hell?"

Shay's words broke up his daydream and caused him to beon alert. She hadn't even backed out of the driveway good before the front door of the house opened and a pretty redbone walked out with Dory close behind her. He had on a pair of boxer shorts and nothing else. He hadn't notice the car that had stopped at the end of the driveway when he slapped the female on her ass, but when she stopped and turned back to him she brought it to his attention.

"Looks like you got some company."

"Oh shit, your red ass better go along with whatever I say."

The woman had always been a conniving bitch but the situation she found herself in was one she wanted to avoid. She knew Dory would make her pay dearly if she didn't go along with his story so she listened intently while he gave her the run down.

"Shay, come on. Can we go?" Dre asked still trying to avoid what would only turn out bad.

"You knew she was in there, didn't you? That's why you were rushing me out of here."

"Come on Shay, I just didn't want you to walk in on it that's all. I don't want to see your heart broke like mine."

"Fuck a broken heart. I'm about to beat that bitches ass."

Shay jumped out of her ride before Dre could stop her and ran up on the woman while Dory stood there and said nothing. He finally moved when Shay punched her but only so she didn't hit him too.

"Bitch, I know you ain't been in there laid up with my fuckin man?"

"Shay, chill baby, it ain't what you think. Come on and give me a chance to explain."

She was too busy beating the woman's ass to pay attention to what Dory was saying. The woman tried her best to fight back but she had used up all her energy fucking Dory for the package he had given her. Shay punched her with as much force as she could muster.

"Fuck it, I'm going back inside." Dory shrugged his shoulders and turned around to go back inside the house. He made sure to close the door behind him.

The woman just could not get out of Shays' grip and was pissed that Dory had abandoned her. She would make him pay for that shit. She continued to try and block the blows that came to her and hoped Shay would eventually grow tired but it was Dre who stopped the show instead.

"Shay, stop. Please. That's my momma."

Chapter 5

"Oh my God, what happened to you?"

"Don't act like you're so concerned with my well being Kayla."

"Ya know what Kiara? I don't understand what's gotten into you. We use to be so close."

"Look, why don't you save that flaw ass bullshit you talking and tell me why you are at my door. I have stuff to do and don't have time for chit chat."

"I came to give you this. For some reason the mailman put it in my box instead of yours," Kayla held out the small envelope that was addressed to Kiara Taylor. She knew what it was, and her heart ached a little knowing that Daymion had put some pretty powerful words inside the letter that the envelope held. She wasn't worried about him getting back with Kiara because she knew that would never happen. She just hated toying with her friend's mind. However, she was willing to try anything if it meant that Dreighton could be treated better.

Kiara looked at the envelope funny and asked, "Who the fuck wrote me?" She then looked in the corner of the envelope and saw the name that was written above the return address. Her heart seem to beat faster and her hands began to shake. She looked up into Kayla's eyes and said, "It's from Daymion."

Kayla had already known where the letter had come from but she played dumb to the fact. "What? You can't be serious. Oh my God, Kiara. I wonder what it says. Open it bitch. What are you waiting for?"

Kiara started to open it but stopped and passed it back to Kayla, "You do it for me."

Kayla could have sworn that she seen a piece of Kiara break and it made her unsure if she should go along with Daymion's plan. Once Kiara found out it was all a lie all hell would break loose. She just prayed that Daymion could keep up his end of the bargain and save his son.

***

Dre couldn't believe that Dory had went out the way he did with his mother, and he was still upset about it. He thought that sets like Dory's held some type of loyalty but obviously that loyalty didn't extend to him. True enough, Dre had a thing for Dory's girl but he hadn't made a move. Now, he would push up on her full force. He told himself that he would leave the crew but he was an asset and Dory wouldn't let him go that easy.

"Nah, lil nigga, you think cause I stuck dick to your crackhead ass momma you just gon break. The fuck is wrong with you?"

"I give you what I owe you every night so what you holding me for? I'm ready to move on and do some other shit. I don't know what the problem is."

Dory chewed on the toothpick he held between his teeth and scoffed. He had to admit, the kid had some balls but his was way bigger. "You don't just join my set and think you can walk away when you want to. Lil nigga, you signed on to this for the rest of your life. Fuck you and your tired ass momma. You belong to me. Now go out there and make me some money."

Dre stood and stared at Dory for a minute. He knew he had put himself in a bad position but his mother had made it even worse. He thought about his options that were few and far between. Dory held out a plastic baggie in **front to** him and Dre finally took it and put it in his pocket. Every time he looked at Dory all he could think about was him and his momma. He shook his head and turned to leave. He walked out the front door so that he could go man the territory he'd been given. As soon as he stepped out on the porch he smiled. He could recognize her scent anywhere and it always caused his dick to stand at attention.

"Hey Dre, where you headed to?"

Shay looked up at his tall frame. He had her beat by a whole foot but to him, she was the perfect height at four feet ten inches tall. He looked down into her eyes and it rumbled his soul to know that she would actually go back to Dory's place after all that had happened. She couldn't have been that naive to believe that he wouldn't ever do it again.

"What choo doing here?"

"I'm just here to see Dory. We made up ya know."

Dre scoffed and shook his head, "He 'ont care about you. If he did he wouldn't have had my momma up in there. That was totally disrespectful and you just gonna let that shit go. The fuck is wrong with you?"

Shay was shocked at the way Dre talked to her because he had always been so respectful. Dory had been the only man she'd ever allowed inside of her so she had never explored any other alternatives. She was still young and he was twice her age but she had other reasons why she was with him that no one else knew of.

"Well Dre, in a relationship when bad things happen, you forgive. I know you don't understand right now but when you find that special someone, you'll do anything to make it work."

"I'm seventeen Shay, not stupid, and I know that he don't deserve you."

"He may not deserve me but right now he is all I got."

"Nah, you got me and I don't plan on ever going anywhere. Come on Shay, just walk away from that nigga. I mean, I know I ain't as high up on the ladder as he is but I'm steady climbing and soon I'm going reach the top. You know I'd treat you right. Just give me a chance to show you."

Before she could respond, a voice came from behind and ruined the moment between them.

"Didn't I tell yo ass not to do all that talking to my workers? Get in the house and let that lil mufucka go handle his business with my shit."

She looked up at Dre one last time. "I'll see you around okay. Be careful out there."

When she was out of earshot, Dory pulled out his gun and cocked it, but little did he know, not even a bullet could keep him from Shay. He would have her no matter what he had to go through to get her.

"Don't get no bright ideas about you and my bitch. A nigga like me ain't just gon step aside and let you slide in so your best bet is to pull the fuck back and don't ever forget that no matter what I do she gon always come back home to daddy."

Dory put his gun back down the waist of his jeans and walked inside leaving Dre, as he stood and thought about what he said, but he would have the last word.

"Don't worry Shay, I ain't going nowhere. I'm a always be there for you. I give you my word, and ain't nobody gonna keep me from honoring it."

***

"You have a collect call from an inmate at a state correctional facility. To accept this call press nine. To refuse press zero."

Kayla pressed nine to accept the call that she had waited on all day.

"Hello Daymion, and before you ask, yes Kiara got the letter."

"So, do you think she fell for it? You think it's gonna work?"

"I just, I know that she was shocked when she saw who it was from. She was so nervous she couldn't even open it. So I had to. I also had to read it to her."

"Okay, so when are y'all coming so I can prepare myself?"

"Daymion, I'm just not sure if I can sit through a visit with you and her. I got some slight feelings for you and just the thought of you even standing close to her makes me sick on my stomach."

Daymion smiled, "Yeah, just some slight feelings. I'm a see if I can change that and make 'em a little stronger."

Kayla blushed on the other end of the line because Daymion Myers sure knew how to worm his way into a woman's heart. She had almost forgot that she was on the telephone until he spoke again.

"Yo, Kayla, did she mention anything about bringing my boy?"

Kayla replied in a disappointed voice, "No, Day. I tried to convince her but she said that she wanted to make sure y'all was gonna work out before she brought Dre. She still doesn't know that I brought him up there. Dre lied and told her that I took him to the arcade."

"Damn, my lil nigga showing some loyalty already," Daymion said while his eyes teared up. He pinched the bridge of his nose so they would remain at bay, not because he was above crying but because he wanted to appear strong for Kayla.

"Yeah, Day. He's such a good kid. I honestly think that all his traits came from you."

They shared a laugh and talked a little longer. They didn't even realize how much time had passed until the phone call cut off on them. Daymion hung up the phone slowly and thought about the visit he was going to have with Kiara. He hadn't seen her since his last day in court over sixteen years ago.

He walked back to his cell so he could get his mind ready. He had to put on his best game face when she showed up. He knew that if anyone could get through to Kiara it would be him and he planned on putting on an Oscar worthy performance.

***

"You act like you feeling that lil nigga or something. Bitch, what's up with that? Ya'll mufukas getting mighty close."

"Really Dory? I don't act any different with him than I do anyone else."

"Well don't forget, you're not his fucking woman, his ass works for me and I don't need you or anyone else distracting him because if he come short with my shit, I'm a put him on his ass."

"Dory, don't you feel bad about putting him on the block? You know it stays hot out there with the cops. Everyone else works out of a house so why don't he? What if something happened to him? Did he tell you about Malice and Kendrick trying to rob him? What if he was your fucking son?"

"Watch your mouth before I wire that bitch shut. His ass came to me looking for work not the other way around and when he told me Daymion Myers was his father, there was no way I could turn him down."

"Daymion Myers? I've heard that name somewhere before."

"Yeah, nigga use to be big on the block but started fuckin with Kiara Taylor when she was only fifteen. He ended up dissin her ass but he had already unknowingly planted his seed. Bitch pressed charges and sent the people on him, nigga just happened to be dirty and the rest is history."

"Hhhmm. It almost seems as if you have some animosity toward him. What happened between you and him?"

The thought of Daymion Myers pissed Dory off. Only a couple of people knew why and Dory wanted to keep it that way.

"How bout you mind your business and stop asking me so many questions that you don't need the answers to. Let me worry about Myers and his son. You just worry about these nuts."

Shay shook her head but did as she was told. She wondered why Dory didn't want to talk about what had happened but she would get to the bottom of it, even if she had to ask Daymion Myers herself.

***

Malice nudged Kendrick with his elbow and pointed at the corner.

"Aye, that mufucka still gon show his ass up out here? He got some fuckin nerve." Kendrick stated.

"I guess he ain't get the message the last time I stepped to him. Come on Kenny, lets go see if we can get it through his head that this spot belongs to us."

Malice began to walk in Dre's direction with Kendrick following close behind. Kendrick was a good kid but his only downfall was that he didn't know how to be a leader. Even when shit didn't feel right to him, he would follow behind Malice. The two eighteen-year-olds had been friends for only about six months and decided that they could make a few dollars by selling crack on the corner of their neighborhood. Malice's older brother use to have men out there but put them all up in trap houses so the corners had been bare. When he told his brother what they wanted to do, he quickly gave them what they needed to get started.

Those same corners belonged to Daymion Myers before he blew up in the street game. He passed them down to Dorian Thompson when he took him under his wing and the rest was history. Dre was serving a customer when the two boys walked up on him.

"Yo, I'll just take that bread off your hands." Malice stated with an outstretched hand.

Dre recognized the voice and thought about his options. He could take off and run but wasn't sure how far he would get or he could stand his ground and face the enemy head on. He finally decided on the latter because if he ran like a coward he would never gain his respect. He thought to himself. It's time to G up. Fuck it. And turned to face the bullies.

"Nah, nigga you gon have to take this bread."

"Oh, so you bad now that you got some new kicks? This our corner and if you wanna keep serving here you gonna have to pay the cost fuck boy."

"Fuck you. Like I said, you gonna have to take this shit tonight cause I ain't giving you nothing."

The two boys laughed at him but said nothing, instead, Malice threw a punch that Dre hadn't been prepared for and knocked him on his ass. When his head hit the concrete he swore that he saw stars, white spots blurred his vision and although, the face in front of him seemed to be spinning, he swung anyway but never landed a punch.

Kendrick hollered from behind Malice as he pounded into Dre's face again. "Get the money out of that niggas pocket and let's go."

He finally stopped when he felt Dre go limp and then took everything out of his front pockets. Malice stood when he heard a vehicle approaching. "I see headlights, let's go. It might be Five-O."

The two of them dipped into the woods just as the vehicle pulled up. Shay screamed and jumped out of her ride. "Oh my God, Dre." She ran to his side and saw that his face was covered in blood and then noticed the bloody rock that lay beside him. His right eye was swollen shut so she immediately pulled out her cell phone and called an ambulance. After she hung up with 911, she dialed Dory's number but got no answer.

"It's okay Dre, I got someone coming to help you."

Once the ambulance arrived and took Dre to the hospital she got back into her ride and followed behind them. Her heart broke in two as she thought about what she had just came up on. She couldn't lie to herself any longer, Dre had stolen her heart but until she finished with what she needed to do; he wouldn't know it.

Dory heard his cell phone ring and so did the woman on top of him. She was riding him reverse cowgirl and he refused to let anything disturb her groove.

"Are you going to answer that?"

"How about you worry about this dick and not who's calling me?"

"It could be your bitch checking up on you."

"Well right now, it seem like you my btich so handle your business."

She placed her hands on his thighs and rode him faster while his phone continued to ring. He finally picked it up so that he could see who the caller was. When he saw it was Shay with a 911 beside her name he sent it to voice mail because to him there was nothing more urgent than this nut he was about to get.

Chapter 6

Kiara was so excited from the words that Daymion had sent her. She couldn't wait until the next morning when Kayla would take her to see her childhood crush. She hadn't even thought about Dre or wondered where he was. He would only be in the way if he were there anyway.

"Yes, this will be perfect. It will remind him about what he's missed," Kiara said out loud while she laid out a pair of Baby Phat jeans on the end of her bed. It would go perfect with the silk blouse she had laid out beside it.

She stripped down to her thongs and bra and then caressed her breasts as she thought about the way Daymion used to suck them. Yeah, she got high from time to time but it never altered her figure. The knocking on the door broke her train of thought. "Dammit," she said and went to answer it.

When she opened the door, Kayla rushed in and said frantically, "Put on some clothes Kiara, Dreighton is in the hospital."

"Okay, well he'll be okay if somethings wrong they'll take care of him. Ain't that what doctors are for? What the hell can I do for him?"

"You could fuckin care. That's what you can do. Now get dressed and let's go."

Kiara put her hands on her hips and said, "Bitch, I got to get ready to go to the club and make some money to pay these damn bills that his ass don't help pay. So, fuck you and him."

"Kiara, how in the hell do you expect him to help you? He don't even have a job and I'm sure if he looked for one he'd be turned away. He's a seventeen-year-old black boy and he's already been stereotyped. That shit ain't easy for him."

"Well it ain't easy for me either. I've held him down by myself ever since he came out of this pussy and now it's time for him to make it on his own. He's old enough to get his ass out on the block like the rest of them do."

"You were supposed to take care of him. You're his mother. What do you think Daymion would say if he knew you treated his son like this?"

"Daymion has no right to worry about Dre. He hasn't even been here his whole life so how he feels about it doesn't matter," Kiara said and walked off to go to her bathroom. Kayla followed close behind.

"Daymion hasn't been here because of you, remember? You're the one that put him where he is now so don't blame him, Kiara. I told you not to fuck with him, but you did anyway. Don't take that shit out on Dre. He don't deserve that."

"Bitch, why you so concerned with my son?" Kiara asked.

"Somebody has to care about him because you damn sure don't."

The slap made contact before Kayla could stop it. She held her palm against the stinging sensation and said, "Bitch, don't you ever put your hands on me again."

Kiara took off her thong and bra and stepped into the shower and asked, "What you gonna do if I do? Not a damn thing. Now get the hell out of my apartment."

"Fine. How about you go suck someone's dick for a ride to see Daymion because I'm not taking your ass anywhere!" Kayla screamed and then stormed out so she could go check on the one thing that mattered most in her life.

***

"Bitch, who the hell are you?" Shay asked when Kayla walked in the room.

"Back down Lassie, this here is my nephew."

"Uh, yeah right. Ain't you the wrong color to be coming up in here claiming a black kid as your nephew. You sure you ain't no detective because he don't have no answers for you and I don't know shit."

"Look, I don't know who the hell you are or even why the hell you're here but don't fuck with me about this boy here. Do you understand?"

Shay started to say something else, but Dre cut her off. "Auntie Kayla, where's my momma?"

"Oh, Dre honey. I'm sorry but she had to go to work and couldn't make it, but I'm here for you," Kayla replied.

When Shay saw the interchange between Dre and Kayla, she felt bad about the way she had treated her. "Look, I'm sorry, I just..."

"It's alright. At least I know that he has someone by his side beside me that gives a fuck about him. What happened?"

"Two dudes jumped on him and robbed him. They took everything he had. I happened to turn the corner and saw him lying on the ground, so I called an ambulance and then followed them here."

Kayla took in what Shay had told her and then said, "Thanks but um, what could they have possibly taken from him to make them beat him up this bad?"

"They took all his money and the rest of the package that Dory had given him. Dory's gonna be pissed but I'll handle him," Shay stated not knowing that Kayla had no clue that Dre had been on the block.

Kayla turned her head and looked at Dre and asked, "Dre when did you start dealing in drugs? What the hell is going on with you? You know better. Your father is going to be so disappointed."

"Well he shouldn't be because I got his blood running through my veins so that makes me a natural born hustler. Besides my momma told me to get out and put in some work so I did as I was told. It don't matter though, because I'm old enough to fend for myself now and that's just what I been doing."

"And yet look where you are at. You should have come to me. I would have never turned you away."

"Nah, Auntie Kay, your place would have been the first place she would have looked. I couldn't put that heat on you. This shit right here is just a minor setback for a major comeback. Those mufuckas gonna pay for what they did to me. I give you my word on that."

Each word that Dre spoke hurt worse than the one before, but he told Kayla the truth. "My momma told me to get out and put in some work because she needed help paying the bills, so I went out and did what she said. I just wanted to make her happy so she would be nice to me, but she just got meaner."

Shay's heart broke and caused her to turn her back to Dre and Kayla. She needed to release the tears that had formed but she didn't want to seem weak. She needed to be strong for Dre because he didn't have any strength of his own. He was broken and she would do whatever it took to piece him back together.

***

"Man, I beat that lil muthafuckas ass just like you paid me to do," Malice said when he walked in the house. He was proud of himself, but Kendrick wasn't feeling it. He knew Malice was savage but that could have been his little brother out there.

"Man, that shit wasn't funny. That kid is probably laid up in the hospital somewhere. Why couldn't you just take his shit without all that?" Kendrick asked.

"Because he did what I told him to do, and that's why his pockets stay laced the fuck up, unlike your broke ass."

Kendrick shook his head in disappointment and said, "Man, I'm outta here. I'll catch you later, Mal." He walked out and slammed the door leaving Malice and his older brother alone. He had never liked his friend's brother so he chose not to stick around when they were together.

"Come on bro, you gotta tell me all about it."

Malice explained it all in detail to his idol. "Man, when we walked up on his lil ass, he acted like he wasn't scared but I swung on his bitch ass. I knocked him on his back and then I let these two muthafuckas pop off." He held up his clenched fists and started punching the air the same way he did Dre's face. He just failed to mention the rock he'd hit him with.

The two shared a laugh at Dre's expense. Malice would do anything for his older brother because he looked up to him like he was a god or something. He wanted to be just like him when he grew up and had been walking in his shoes ever since he took his first step.

"Man, you did good and even if you wasn't my brother, I'd still fuck with you." The two gave each other dap and shared a blunt as they continued to talk about what had happened. They were so engrossed in their conversation that they didn't hear the front door open. Shay stood there and listened as the two plotted another hit on Dre. She couldn't believe that Dory had his little brother jumping on Dre and robbing him. She told herself that there was no way she could continue seeing him after what she'd heard. She knew that Dory was cold but to have him beaten up was beyond anything she could ever imagine him doing. She knew that it would be hard to get out of his grasp, but she would figure it out.

All she could worry about at that moment was Dre laid out in the hospital and had did nothing wrong. She decided that she was going to pay Daymion Myers a visit because she wanted to get to the bottom of the beef with them. In the meantime, she would play along with Dory. She finally made her presence known and walked in the room and asked, "What's so funny?"

Dory looked up when he heard Shay's voice. Both him and Malice got quiet not knowing that they had already been heard. Shay walked over to Dory and sat on his lap and said in a whisper, "Baby, my pussy is so wet. Can you send him away so we can be alone?"

Dory smiled and his dick instantly got hard. No matter how many other women he fucked behind Shay's back, he still stayed ready for her.

"Yo lil bro, you gots to get out here. I'll holla at you in a little while," Dory said to Malice.

Malice had never cared too much for Shay. He always believed that she was a gold digger. She was only a couple of months older than him and felt like Dory should find someone else close to his age. Little did he know the feelings were mutual. He gave Shay a dirty look and got up from the chair and said, "Aight bro, I'll see you."

Once they were alone, Shay stripped down to nothing and watched as Dory did the same. She couldn't believe that the man in front of her had someone beaten up and knew that if he would do it to Dre, he would do it to anybody. Shay was going to fuck him really good and then when he was wore out, she would wait till he went to sleep and take what she could until she felt that it was enough. However, she wasn't going to take the money and drugs for herself. She was getting it for Dre and to her, he deserved it all.

***

Kiara sat at the visiting table and bit the inside of her cheek. She looked around the room at the other inmates who were there with visits and wondered what their stories were like. Did the mother of their children put them away too? All she wanted was Daymion Myers and if he would have just gone along with her plan for them to be together, he never would have done one day in prison. It wasn't her fault he had drugs on him when they arrested him.

She was so deep in her thoughts that she didn't feel the presence in front of her.

"Hey, yo, Kiara, you aight?"

His voice still made her panties wet and she closed her eyes to enjoy that moment of bliss. She felt as if it was a dream and she never wanted to wake up but then, the voice came again.

"Yo, Kiara. Kiara, what's up?"

She opened her eyes and stared at the object of her desire. If she hadn't been in a public setting, she would have stripped all her clothes off and jumped on the form in front of her. He was still the most handsome man she had ever seen. Kiara had never been one to be at a loss for words, but she couldn't form one sentence.

"Kiara, you just gonna sit there and stare at me or you gon' stand up and let a nigga put his arms around something familiar?"

"Oh, I'm so sorry. Hello, Daymion."

Kiara stood up as he had asked and let the father of her son wrap his arms around her. It was a feeling of euphoria, and she didn't want him to ever let her go. There had been many men after Daymion but none of them could give her body the chills that he did.

When the embrace was cut short by a guard, Kiara wanted to curse him out but she didn't want Daymion to see the other side of her. She sat back down and waited because she knew that the questions were about to begin. The look Daymion gave her felt like one of lust and desire but to him it was a look of disgust.

Kiara will still thick and fine, but he could see how the years that passed had worn on her. She looked older than her thirty two years, but her beauty still could be seen. He held so much animosity toward the woman in front of him but had to put on a show for the sake of his seed. He wondered how she had gotten there. He had hoped that Kayla would change her mind and bring her but instead, she stuck to her word. That seemed to turn him on even more because he liked a woman who could stand her ground.

"It's so good to see you, Kiara, and even after all these years, you still as pretty as the first day I met you."

Kiara blushed like a teenager in love and said, "Thanks, Day. You still got it too. I'm sorry for putting you through this but you didn't give me much of a choice."

"Nah, I've forgiven you but why didn't you let me be a part of Dreighton's life? As a matter of fact, why didn't you bring him? How is he?"

Kiara's lies came quick and easy. "Oh, he's so wonderful, Day and he looks just like you. I didn't bring him because I wanted to make sure that this would go good between us. I didn't want to get his hopes up. I'll consider bringing him next time, okay. Let's make this visit just about us."

"Please just tell me something." Daymion pleaded but it was another voice that answered him.

"She can't tell you Daymion because she doesn't know the answers," Kayla said from behind.

Daymion was pissed that Kayla was going to ruin his plan, but he had to maintain his composure.

"Um, what the fuck are you doing here?" Kiara asked with an attitude.

"I'm here to stop your lies, Kiara. Why don't you tell Daymion that his son was laid up in a hospital bed for two days because he was out there selling dope and got beat up by two other boys?"

Daymion stood from his seat and asked, "What the fuck did you just say? My boy is out there selling dope?"

"She's lying, Day. I don't even know why she's here."

"I'm sorry, Day but there was no way I could let you go through with this visit. You needed to know the truth."

"Dammit Kayla, just sit down and shut the hell up and let me handle this." He stated as calmly as he could. He knew Kayla had his best interest at heart but she had also ruined his plan.

Kiara sucked her teeth and stood. "I know you didn't bring your white ass here to try and sabotage my relationship with Daymion. But I guess I shouldn't have expected anything less because you have always been jealous of me."

"Jealous of what Kiara? Of all the men you go through on a weekly basis? And as far as your relationship with Daymion goes, bitch you don't have one and never will."

The guard heard the commotion going on and walked over to their table "Myers, you need to get your visitors under control because they are disturbing the others. If you can't then they'll have to leave."

The two women heard what the guard had said and grew quiet, but Kiara was the first to break the silence. "Don't worry I'm leaving. Daymion, you can kiss my ass and your son's goodbye. And Kayla, you no longer have a friend. I'm outta here."

Kiara turned and walked away and left Daymion and Kayla standing there. She couldn't believe that she had almost gotten played again. She was more determined than ever to keep Dre away from his father even if she had to pack him up and send him away. She was gonna up her clientele so she could make enough money to move. She just hoped that she could stay off the pipe long enough to save it.

***

"Yo Trap, you been going in my pot nigga?" Dory asked when he noticed that money had been going missing. He also noticed that his premade packages were short too.

"The fuck you asking me some shit like that for?" Trap Town asked.

"Nigga, because I can," Dory stated angrily.

"You should be asking your little brother that question. Shit ain't start going missing until you started letting his ass hang around."

About that time, Teddy walked in with Dre following behind him. Dory made sure that Malice didn't come around that day because he didn't want Dre to know that he had been the one setting him up, but Dory didn't know that Shay had already put him up on game, and Dre would never rat Shay out.

"Dory, look what I got here. Lil Spade out the hospital and shit. His ass ready to get back out there too," Teddy stated proudly. He had grown close to the boy and wasn't aware of the hatred Dory held in his heart for his father, Daymion Myers.

"Okay, lil nigga, you sho' you ready because I can't afford to keep losing bread because your ass weak and can't defend yourself."

I ain't weak. Those punks just keep catching me off guard. They fuckin cowards so they come at me from behind and by the time I see them, it's too late. Those pussies are the ones who's weak."

"Punks, huh. Yeah, well you better not lose not another dime of my shit. You do understand that, don't you?"

"Yeah, Dory, I understand and I ain't gonna let them niggas catch me slippin no more."

"Yeah, well we gon' see."

Dory hadn't mentioned anything else about his money and drugs coming up short. His focus now was on the boy in front of him. He planned on sending Malice back out on the corner again to rob young Dre. He wanted the kid in his debt so far that he couldn't get out so when his fuck ass daddy came home, he would have to pay the price over his son's head. He knew that he would have an advantage over Daymion Myers because the nigga had been out of the loop for a while, and it would take him a minute to build himself back up. By the time he did, it would be too late. Dory was the head nigga now and he'd suffer a slow death before he'd allow Daymion to take that away from him.

Meanwhile, on the other side of town things weren't going so great for Mellow. By the time he saw the blue and red lights, it was too late to get away. They were on him so quick that he couldn't even get rid of the product in his pocket.

"Don't move motherfucker," the officer stated while he pointed his gun at Mellow who held his hands up in surrender. He knew that the police wouldn't hesitate to kill a black man so he did as he was told and hoped that his life would be spared.

"Do you have any weapons on your person that we need to know about?" The other officer asked.

"Yeah, I got a piece under my shirt but I ain't trying to have a gun play with y'all. I will not reach for the weapon," Mellow stated.

The officer said, "Turn around slowly with your hands up and face the wall."

Mellow did as instructed and once he had his back to them, he placed his palms against the brick wall. He thought of all the black lives that had been lost at the hands of the police and said a small prayer.

"I am coming up behind you to search your body so don't make any unexpected moves. If you do, my partner will not hesitate to shoot. Do you understand?"

"Yes, sir," Mellow said as his heartbeat faster.

The officer patted Mellow down and found a weapon, drugs and money that Dory was going to be pissed about, but there was nothing Mellow could do. He never thought a day like that would happen. Although, he knew the consequences of the life he chose to live.

"Put your hands behind your back, Mr. Odom. You're going to jail this time. You have the right to remain silent, anything you say can and will…"

"I know. I know. You don't gotta say the whole speech! Just take me in so I can call my fuckin lawyer," Mellow stated in a disappointed voice.

Once Mellow was in the back of the police car, the two officers shared a high five. They had been trying to catch Mellow off guard for a minute now, but he had always been up on his game. He wasn't the big fish but he was enough.

Mellow sat in the backseat and thought about his momma. He knew that Dory only gave a fuck about himself so he couldn't ask him to look out for her. He decided that his one phone call would be to Big Gun because he knew he wouldn't be home for a minute and his friend had a heart of gold. He told himself that when he got out of this, he would change his life and try to find something more legit but

Mellow was born and bred a dope boy. It was all he knew how to do.

When the car pulled away from the curb and turned a corner, he looked out the window and locked eyes with young Dre, and wondered just how long Dory would keep the kid out there because when Daymion Myers found out, there would be hell to pay. He didn't want to be in the crossfire when it happened because he knew someone would be paying with their life and it wasn't going to be him.

Chapter 7

Kayla sat and bit her nails to the meat. She knew that she had fucked up when she walked in on Kiara and Daymion's visit. She didn't care about Day being mad at her, she just couldn't let him go through with his plan. She was too afraid that it would backfire. She only hoped that she didn't make it worse for Dre.

When her phone rang, she jumped up and answered it quickly. She didn't even let the operator finish her speech before she pressed the number that would make the call go through.

"Daymion, I'm so sorry. Oh my God, I didn't think you were ever gonna call me again," Kayla pleaded before Daymion had a chance to speak.

"Yo, you know you fucked up, right? How the hell you gonna hold a nigga down pulling bullshit like that? The fuck is wrong with you?" He asked.

"I don't know, Daymion. After I thought about it, I couldn't let you go through with it. I know that I was being selfish. I just hope you can forgive me."

"Nah, you weren't being selfish, your ass was just plain stupid. What if she runs off with my fuckin son? I can't believe that shit happened."

"Daymion, I promise I won't pull nothing like that again. I give you my word."

"Your word, huh? Well, answer this question for me, while you are sitting on the phone talking to me, where the hell is my son?"

Kayla was stuck and couldn't answer his question because honestly, she had no clue where Dre was at. She knew that he had been released from the hospital but that was it. Daymion waited a minute and gave her time to answer but when she didn't say anything he said, "That's what the fuck I thought," and hung up.

***

Dre stood and thought about what he had just seen. He wondered how long it would take before word got back to Dory about Mellow's arrest. He thought about running back to the house and telling him but making his money seemed a little more important. He then turned his head and faced the voice coming at him.

"Hey, hey, little guy. You think you could front me a twenty. I'll come back by in an hour and pay you. I just got to go turn this trick real quick. What do you say?"

Dre had never seen anything more horrific in his life. The female that asked him for credit had matted hair and cracked lips. Her eyes were as big as saucers and bulged from her face. He was sure that if she took her shirt off, he could count her ribs because she was so skinny. He wondered who could be dumb enough to do anything sexual with her.

"Nah, I got to have my money up front. I can't be doing no credits."

"Ah, come on now, little man. I can do something for you if you like. Shit, you ain't never too young to get some head. They say I suck a mean dick," The woman said and inched closer to him but a vehicle pulled up before she got too close.

"Tammy, what the hell you doing out here? I know you ain't trying that boy."

"Ah, come on Teddy. Somebody gotta teach him the ropes."

"Well, it damn sure ain't gonna be you. Now get your ass outta here and leave him alone."

"Ah come on, Teddy. I just need a couple hits till later on," She stated and stepped close to his ride.

"Nah, you ain't getting no credit here and you damn sure ain't sucking my dick. Come on, Spade, get in before your lil ass fuck around and get molested out here."

Dre hurriedly jumped in the truck thankful that he had been rescued from the crackhead. He wondered what was up with Teddy coming his way and hoped that he wasn't in trouble with Dory.

"Thanks Teddy, but what are you doing this way?" He asked.

Teddy glanced at him and then put his eyes back on the road and said, "My sister asked me to come out here and get you."

"Why? You know I can't go back without making Dory's money."

"I'm about to teach you how to survive."

"What you mean, teach me to survive? I was born for these streets. 'Nigga do you know who my pops is? I just need a weapon and some ammo for them punks! I ain't a little boy, I can guide myself."

"Yeah and ya ass ain't fully grown yet either. Just cause your daddy was a legend don't make you a solider. There's more to the game than standing on corners and carrying a gun, besides, my sister is worried about you."

"Fuck that. Her ass ain't too worried because if she was she wouldn't keep running back to fuck boy."

"Someone sounds jealous but don't worry. She has motive. Just sit back and keep playing your hand and eventually you'll pull the right card."

"You think so because I ain't feeling so confident right now."

"Don't worry playa, just let her handled her biz."

Dre hoped Teddy was right because behind every real Boss was a real bitch and Shay was the only one for him.

"Don't worry about that, aight. Me and Shay got you covered on that end. Right now, you coming to our crib and we gonna teach you how to survive out here. Dory ain't even gonna know you gone and ain't gonna give a fuck as long as you show up with his money," Teddy stated.

Malice walked through the cut so that he could walk up on Dre and take his stash again. He was pissed because Kendrick told him that he wasn't going along with beating him up anymore. "Ole soft ass nigga," Malice said out loud as if Kendrick could hear him. He didn't need his friend to help him jump the boy. He just needed him to watch his back in case the police rolled up but fuck it. He would just be more alert.

When he got to the end of the path, he saw Tammy talking to Dre and already knew what it was about because Tammy tried everybody. She would do anything for a hit. He was about to step out of the cut when Teddy pulled up and scooped Dre up in his ride. He wondered if his brother knew that Dre had been taken from the spot that he assigned him to. Malice knew that something was up, he just didn't know what. He decided to turn around and head to the trap house so he could stir up some shit, but before he could make it back through the cut, he ran in to the person who was supposed to have his back.

Malice didn't know what had hit him, but it knocked him right off his feet. After his head cleared, he opened his eyes and saw a familiar face.

"Man, Kendrick, what the fuck's up?"

"That shit hurt, didn't it muthafucka?" Kendrick asked.

"Dawg, what's up with you? Why you do that shit man?"

"I did it to show you that you ain't that damn tough. What happened with all that shit you was talking earlier? Huh, bitch?" Kendrick kicked Malice in the ribs and stomach after each question. He was tired of being bullied by Malice and decided it was time to even the score. He had never wanted to go along with the things that Malice did but the threat of answering to Dory always made him give in.

"Nigga my brother gonna kill your fuck ass for this," Malice said through clenched teeth as pain shot through his body.

"Oh yeah. Well, tell your brother he can suck my dick. As a matter of fact, tell his bitch ass to drink this." Kendrick pulled his dick out and pissed all over Malice while he tried to curl up into a ball. When he was done, he shook his dick off and put it back in his pants and said, "When you and Dory ready for some, come holla at me. I'll be waiting."

Kendrick already knew that Malice wasn't going to say anything to Dory because he would be too embarrassed to admit that he got his ass beat by someone he thought was weaker than him. Malice waited till he thought Kendrick was gone and got up from where he lay. He was pissed and the only thing on his mind was payback. He already knew how he was going to get it.

***

Big Gun answered his phone on the first ring but what came from the other end wasn't what he expected. "You have a collect call from Montell Banks. If you accept the charges, press one now."

Big Gun pressed the one on his keypad and listened to Mellow's voice as it came through the line. "Yo Big G, my nigga I just got popped. I think I'm going up this time man. Them crackers got all my shit. I ain't even had a chance to drop."

Big Gun sat up and put his elbows on his knees. He didn't know what to say but he knew he had to say something, "Damn, dawg, how the fuck you get caught slippin' like that? The fuck was you thinking?"

"I 'ont know, G. A nigga like me always stay on point but I ain't see that shit coming."

"I suppose you want me to tell Dory this shit. Damn, that muthafucka gonna trip."

"Yeah I already called my lawyer, but he said I'm gonna do some time no matter what. I had a piece on me. That's five off top."

Big Gun could hear the sorrow in his partner's voice and it saddened him. He knew that Mellow was strong minded but even the strongest niggas didn't want to sit behind the wall. Big Gun knew that deals would be offered and that would cause things to get ugly real quick. He also knew that Mellow was a thorough ass nigga but even the strongest had fallen victim to the good cop bad cop routine.

"Yo man, don't let them crackers play your ass out. You hear me?"

"Nah man. I'm a lay down and take this shit like a soldier. Y'all ain't gotta worry. Just promise me that you'll look out for my ole girl. Make sure she straight. This shit gonna break her heart man."

"Now you know I love her like she my own momma, so you don't gotta worry about that. Keep me up on your court dates and shit. I got you, man, I'm a ride it with you."

"Thanks, Gun. Nigga, that's why I fucks with you. Tell Dory he's straight. Just have me ready when I walk out them gates, aight."

"Aight, Mel. Peace, man," Big Gun said and hung up. He put his shoes on so he could walk the path to where Dory was. He knew that Dory stayed paranoid and news like this would make it worse. He hoped that Mellow kept his word and rode like the soldier he claimed to be because if he didn't his ole girl wouldn't need to be looked after because she'd be six feet deep.

***

Dory was deep in some random chick's pussy when the door opened. He looked up and saw that it was Big Gun, so he kept pounding into the wetness in front of him.

"Damn nigga, your ass don't know how to knock?"

"Shit shoulda been locked my nigga. The fuck you woulda done if I'd been Shay coming through the door?"

"Man, what you mean? I would've let Shay suck this bitch cum off of this muthafucka. That's what I woulda done. Shay don't run shit. Just give me a minute G." Dory closed his eyes and suddenly stopped his rhythm. His ass cheeks clenched tightly as he released his load into the woman in front of him.

When he was done, he pulled his dick out, peeled the condom off and told her, "Come on and clean this shit up." He sat down and the woman instantly got up and kneeled on the floor in front of him so she could do as he said.

Big Gun shook his head, "Nigga, you silly as fuck."

"Man, you want some? That pussy nice and wet," Dory said while he pushed the woman's head down on his manhood. Dory was foul when it came to women and treated them all of them the same. He thought they were only good for making his dick wet and nothing else.

Big Gun replied, "Nah, D. I'm gonna pass on that. I am not about to stick my shit in no bitch behind you."

"So, what you saying nigga?"

"I'm saying hell no. Ain't no telling what you shooting outta that bitch, condom or not." Big Gun said and pointed to Dory's dick.

Dory didn't take what Big Gun said as an insult because they had always shot the bullshit like that. It was not the first time that they had a conversation while Dory was being serviced but Big Gun knew that as soon as he said what he came there to say, Dory's dick would go limp as a noodle.

"Yo man, what's up though? You look like you got some shit on your mind."

Big Gun finally said, "Yo D, Mellow got popped a few hours ago that's why we ain't seen him. He down at county right now."

Dory pushed the woman off of him and stood up. He grabbed his jeans off the back of the couch and pulled out some money and threw it on the table in front of the woman and said, "Take that shit and get your ass outta here."

The woman grabbed the money and hurriedly got dressed. When she left the room, Dory turned to Big Gun and asked, "The fuck you mean he got popped?"

"He was off his game and getting ready to bring it in and them crackers came outta nowhere. He ain't have time to take care of his shit before they had him."

"How much shit you talkin' about?"

"Man, Mellow was laced. He had his piece on him too," Big Gun said disappointingly.

"Fuck. That piece is a hard nickel itself. Them crackas gonna come with a deal and try to get him to open up."

"D, you 'ont gotta worry man. Mellow solid as steel. That nigga gonna lay for his. He ain't never been a pussy like that. You good."

Dory knew that Mellow had always claimed to be solid, but he had never been popped on gun and drug charges. It had always been petty bullshit. Now, he was playing in the major leagues, so Dory wasn't convinced. He asked Big Gun, "Yo, Mel already talked to the lawyer? Ain't their something he could do to get outta this? I mean that nigga ain't never had those types of charges. Man, I ain't sure that his ass ain't gonna break."

Big Gun replied, "Yo, Dory, come on, man. Mel been in shit before and he held it down."

"Yeah, but he ain't never been in shit this deep."

"Just chill, D. My boy gonna lay. You ain't got to worry. He said just have him right when he gets out so he can get back up. Aight."

"Yeah, well I hope you know what you talkin' about because if that nigga fold, I'm gonna get his ass where it hurts."

***

Malachi Jenson liked what he saw in front of him. "Man, that bitch can have all my bread," he said to his best friend, Cardo while he watched the fat ass pop in front of him. He imagined his hands on it while the bitch it belonged to rode him slowly. He wondered if she had a man but then decided that he really didn't give a fuck because she was going to be his one way or the other.

"Damn nigga, you look like you already in love and you ain't even had the pussy," Cardo said and nudged his friend arm.

Malachi paid his friend no mind and kept his focus on the redbone in front of him until her set was over. When she left the stage, he felt a great sense of loss. He got up from his seat and went to find the woman who had captured him.

Cardo asked, "Where you going man? They 'bout to bring two bitches up there together."

Malachi shook his head and said, "I'm going to find my future bitch."

He walked up to the bouncer and asked, "Aye yo man, could you tell me where that thick ass redbone just went?"

The bouncer looked at him like he was crazy and said, "What's it in for me?"

Malachi pulled out a wad of cash and passed the man three bills and said, "Now go get what I asked for." The bouncer quickly pocketed the cash and walked off. Malachi stood by and waited patiently until the man came back.

"Yo, come follow me," The bouncer said when he reappeared.

Malachi did as he said and was taken to the door of a private room.

"She's all yours," The bouncer stated and walked away.

Malachi opened the doors slowly and peeked inside. The redbone looked at him and said, "You scared."

He finally walked in the room and quietly shut the door behind him. She asked, "Come on, you wanted a private dance, didn't you?" I don't have all night. There's more money out there."

The closer he got to her, the more his heartbeat sped up and when he was finally directly in front of her, he felt like he was going into cardiac arrest. She giggled and pushed him down into the chair so she could put on a winning performance. She walked to the table and turned on the song Rocket and lip synced the words coming out of the speakers.

"Let me put this ass on it. Show you how it feels."

She slowly grinded her hips as Beyonce's voice continued to fill the room.

"*Let me take this off, watch me,*" The redbone untied the small top that covered the most beautiful breasts Malachi had ever seen. Her nipples hardened as soon as the air hit them but instead of a sense of pleasure, all Malachi could feel was jealousy.

He thought about the many other men she had danced for. He wondered how many times she had used this same song to grind on a nigga's dick. He looked deep in her eyes right before she turned her back to him and bent over to slide her panties down. Her wetness glistened in the dim light, and he didn't even want to imagine how many men had felt it. He didn't want to scare her, but he had to erase the thoughts before he became angry.

Malachi stood from the chair and grabbed her arm. He pulled her close to him and said, "Go tell your boss you quit. You coming with me."

She didn't know how to respond to what he had said and tried to pull away from him but the harder she tried, the more nervous she became, and he could sense her fear.

He said, "Don't worry. I ain't trying to hurt you. I like you and I'm just trying to get to know you better, but I can't have a woman who is in here showing what belongs to me to everyone else."

His words softened her heart although, she didn't know him. She asked, "You don't even know me. What makes you think that you can just come up in here and claim me? Who the hell do you think you are?"

He raised an eyebrow and then let her arm go. He wanted her to see that she was safe with him. "I'm Malachi Jensen and I know you heard of me. I apologize for scaring you but the thought of you doing all this for another man makes me wanna go out there and start shootin'. I'm trying to have all this to myself, so what's up."

His boldness turned her on, she had heard his name before and heard that he was a real boss. Bitches would give up everything to be on his arm but she needed her job even though she only danced a few times a month because she had bills to pay and no one to help her do it. She thought about what he'd said but was still a little skeptical.

She asked, "What if I don't want to quit my job? Maybe I like shaking my ass for all those men."

Malachi's nose flared at her words. He was determined to cuff her and wasn't leaving the strip club without her even if he had to use force. "Fuck that. I'm the only nigga you gonna be shakin' that ass for from now on."

"Nigga, fuck you. I got bills to pay and right now, this is what's paying them."

Malachi pulled out his wad of cash again but this time he handed over the entire stack and said, "After tonight, you ain't gonna have no more bills so you comin' with me or what?"

She didn't know how much money he had just placed in her hand, but she was sure that it was a lot more than she'd ever held in her life. She figured that she had nothing to lose and a nigga with bread was just what she needed. She looked into his eyes and said, "Give me a minute to go get my things. I'll tell my boss on the way out." She then headed to the door and opened it but before she walked out the room, Malachi asked one more thing from her.

"Aye shawty, I forgot to ask. What's your name?"

The redbone answered, "It's Kiara." and then she shut the door behind her.

Chapter 8

"So, why you brought me here? Does Dory know you messin' up his money?" Dre asked.

Teddy looked at him crazy and said, "Lil nigga, you sho' ask a lot of damn questions? The fucks up with that?"

"I'm just trying to make it to my birthday next month that's all. If I don't have Dory's money, that might not happen."

Teddy laughed and said, "Don't worry. Your ass gonna make it. Come on, my sister's waiting on us."

Teddy opened his car door and got out, but Dre stopped him, "I'm gonna marry Shay's pretty ass when I get my status up."

"The hell you are. Ain't no way I'm putting up with your ass for that damn long."

They shared a laugh and got out of the car. Any stranger walking by would mistake the two for father and son because of the closeness the two had formed. Teddy knew that young Dre was sweet on his sister but Dre had some more growing up to do before he could even think about a girl like Shay.

"Damn Teddy, what took y'all so long? Hey Dre, I hope you're hungry because I made enough food for the whole block," Shay said when she opened the door for them.

Dre replied, "I'm always hungry for anything coming from you."

Teddy shook his head and then went to the bathroom to wash his hands with Dre following behind him.

"Yo, you gonna stay here for a couple of days because there's some shit me and my sister gonna teach you about the game you in. I know your pops been gone for a minute and aint been around to guide you but they say he's the best to ever do it so all of it should come natural. Do you need to call your momma or something so they know you safe?"

"Man, my damn momma probably don't even know I'm gone. I'm good but what about Dory?"

"Nigga, fuck Dory. We gonna make sure you still show up and get your packages and we gonna make sure you show back up to pay him but you ain't going back out on that corner until you can defend yourself against his little brother."

"His little brother? Man Teddy, what the hell you talking about?"

"That lil nigga that's been jumping on you is Dory's brother. He been paying him to do that shit, and he's gonna keep doing it because he wants you in debt to him and as long as Malice keeps taking the money you make, the more you gonna owe."

Dre couldn't believe what he had heard. He thought Dory was helping him, but he was using him instead. He wondered how Teddy knew.

"How you know all this? You in on it or something? Beside I don't owe his ass shit. I pay him every night." Dre asked.

"If I was in on it, your ass wouldn't be here right now. What's up? You wanna learn something about the street game or you want me to take you back out there so you can wait on Malice to beat that ass?"

"You could've left me there. I'm ready for his ass. I been practicing in my room at night," Dre said and held up his fists like he was going to punch somebody.

"Yeah, come on then. Take your best shot," Teddy said and turned his head to the side pointing to his jaw line.

"Uh, I hope y'all are done. Dinners getting cold," Shay said from the doorway.

Dre put his fists down, "You lucky. She just saved you from getting a few bruises."

"Oh yeah, well we can take this outside after we eat," Teddy said playfully.

"Nah, I'm gonna have to let me food settle but thanks for the offer."

Teddy, Shay and Dre sat around the table like a real family. Something that Dre had never experienced. He was thankful that these people had come into his life but he knew that he would have to return to the hell that he lived in eventually because the devil wouldn't let him stay away for long.

***

"Myers, let's go. You got a visit."

Daymion could not believe his ears. He knew that it couldn't be anyone, but Kayla knew he was still pissed at her.

"Man, this girl ain't just gonna leave shit alone," Daymion said while he put on his shoes and shirt.

Branch asked, "Look dawg. I ain't trying to tell you what to do but maybe you should hear her out. I really think she has your best interest at heart."

"Fuck my best interest. I need to know my son is straight and she could have jeopardized any future I had with him," Daymion said and walked out to go face the woman he thought he would spend his future with.

Kayla's nervousness went away as soon as she saw him enter the room. She just couldn't believe that she had fucked up so early in what they were building together. She was willing to do anything to win back his trust. When he made it to the table, she stood and walked around the table to meet him. When he pulled her into his arms, she knew that she still had a chance to make things right.

"You know I'm pissed off at you, right?" Daymion stated while he looked down and into her saddened eyes.

Kayla nodded, "Yeah Day, I know you are and you should be. I fucked up and I am so sorry but I just couldn't let you go through with that you had planned. I don't know. I just feel like you would have really regretted it."

When their embrace ended, they sat down at the table across from each other and Daymion asked exactly what Kayla knew he would. "Have you seen my boy?" However, he felt like he already knew the answer.

Kayla said disappointingly, "No Daymion, I haven't seen him which means that Kiara probably hasn't seen him either. I've waited for his knock on the door in the middle of the night, but it hasn't come. I'm sorry."

Daymion rested his head in the palm of his hands and became more pissed off than what he was. He wanted to curse Kayla out and tell her never to return but he needed her because she was his only connection to his son. He would drag her along while he was in there but if she wanted a real future with him, she would have a lot of proving to do because the last thing he needed was a jealous disloyal bitch on his team.

The next few weeks went by without any drama. During those weeks, Teddy taught Dre all he needed to know about the life he had chosen to live. Dre was happy that he hadn't been forced to go out on the block, but he also knew that eventually he would have to show his face. At least, he'd be ready for Malice and Kendrick when they showed up.

He'd be eighteen in another year but his dope boy demeanor made him feel like he was older. He had been going back and forth from Teddy and Shay's to his momma's apartment. However, every time he went home his momma was nowhere to be found. It saddened him even more to think that she hadn't even bothered to look for him. He thought about the last time he was there. He had run into his Auntie Kayla.

"Oh my God, Dreighton, where the hell have you been? Your father has been asking about you."

"Have you seen my momma?" Dre asked ignoring what Kayla said to him.

"No, Dre. I haven't seen Kiara in a couple of weeks. I knew you wasn't with her because the last time I saw her she was with some man I'd never seen before. She went in and picked up a few things and was gone again. Where have you been? Are you okay?"

Dre was silent for a minute and asked, "When are you going to see my daddy again?"

"I'm going next weekend. Do you wanna come with me?"

He thought about her question and then said, "Nah, I'm gonna get Shay to take me. I'll see you around, Auntie Kayla." He turned around to leave but stopped after a few steps. He dug in his pocket and turned back around to face her. "If you see my momma again, give her this." He handed Kayla a wad of cash and then walked away.

***

"Bitch, it's been you this whole time?" Dory asked when he walked in the room. He had caught Shay red handed. He had never suspected her cause he thought she had more sense than to fuck with his stash.

"No, Dory. I just needed a few dollars that's all. This is the first time I've done it." Dory knew that Shay was aware of the money and drugs that were going missing so for her to play dumb pissed him off even more.

The first punch knocked her on her back. "Bitch, you sucking that glass dick now?"

"No Dory. I swear this is my first time in your stash. You gotta believe me."

She felt a rib crack when his steel toed Timberlands made contact. He then bent down and pulled her up by her shirt and punched her again. She swore her jaw had broken. The tears blinded her view of him but she didn't have to see him to feel his fist seal her eye shut.

"I'm a teach your ass about fuckin with my shit, and don't let me find out you did it for that nigga. You think I'm stupid but I know you got a thing for him."

"No Dory, your wrong, I only wanna be with you and I'll pay you back every penny. I swear I will."

"You stupid bitch." He hollered and landed another punch.

Shay had seen Dory angry before and knew what he was capable of so she used the only thing she thought she could to soften him up. "Dory, stop. You're going to hurt the baby."

He paused and looked at her like she was the one who was crazy and asked, "What baby? What the hell you talking about, Shay? Quit fucking playing with me."

"Dory, were gonna have a baby. I'm pregnant," Shay replied.

Dory thought about what she said for a minute. He had always wanted a child. A son that could continue his bloodline. He had almost had one but a bullet to the neck took the life of the woman who was carrying him, and it had changed Dory forever.

He wasn't sure if Shay was telling him the truth or if she was just saying it to make him stop. He looked in Shay's eyes and wondered where her respect for him had went. He pondered on the thoughts of their future together and wondered if they could even have one now. No matter how many bitches he fucked, he still felt like she was the one.

"A baby?"

Shay nodded and said in a sincere voice, "Yeah Dory, were gonna have a baby. I found out this morning. You're gonna be a daddy."

Shay swore that she could feel his heart soften. He let her hair go and she felt the pressure ease. Her eye throbbed in pain and she could only hope that he was done with the tirade. She watched him put his dick back in his pants and then turned his back to her. Shay slowly got up from the floor and grabbed her T-shirt to cover herself back up. Although, Dory had seen her naked flesh many times she somehow felt ashamed.

"A fucking baby?" Dory asked again but instead of Shay responding, she walked up behind him and wrapped her arms around his waist. Dory shut his eyes and saw visions of Malia. He could see her clear as day, and then he saw red. He turned around to face Shay and rubbed a finger over her swollen eye. He thought about the baby she claimed to be carrying and decided that he didn't believe her and there was only one was to know for sure if she was telling the truth.

He kissed her and then pushed her softly against the wall and backed away from her. Shay looked at him seductively and pulled the T-shirt back off. She knew that the news of her being pregnant would do something to Dory and she thought telling him was the only thing that would save her.

"You say we having a baby, huh?"

She smiled and rubbed her stomach and said, "Yes Dory. I know you've wanted a child for a while. You're going to be a wonderful father."

"Nah, I ain't about to have no child with a disloyal bitch." Then, he punched her in the stomach.

Shay grabbed her belly as the blood flowed down her thighs. She couldn't believe that he had did that. She thought he would have been happy but instead, he had destroyed the only thing she had as leverage.

"No Dory, the baby. You gotta take me to the hospital. I'm losing the baby," Shay cried out and slid down the wall. She was too weak to do anything else.

"Bitch you thought telling me you were going to have my baby would make me go soft on your ass? Huh? You took from me and had me believing it was one of my crew the entire time. I thought better of you but you ain't shit to me no more. Now, get your bloody ass outta my shit and don't ever show your face around here again. Before you leave, make sure you clean that bastard you lost off my carpet," Dory said and then walked out and slammed the door behind him.

Shay laid there in a fetal position and thought about the child that Dory had just taken from her. She never thought that he would stoop to that level but she knew she had some karma coming for what she had been doing. Dory had given her all she could dream of and yet she was still so miserable, but the baby could have been what she needed to be happy.

"Somebody help. Please help me. My baby. Please help my baby," Shay cried out in a whisper. She thought about her brother and knew that he would seek revenge. She wanted to tell him not to because she deserved what she got. If she had never stolen from Dory, she would still have her baby. Then, her thoughts turned to Dre, she had so much love for him and hoped to one day have a future with him. She stole the money to help him pay Dory so he wouldn't be in debt. She couldn't believe that Dory was sending Malice out to jump on him. "I'm so sorry Dre," Her tears blinded her yet, she was in too much pain to wipe them away. Her mind told her to get up and get to a phone so she could call for help but before she could act on it, everything went black.

***

Malachi had his dick so deep in Kiara she swore she could feel it in her chest.

"Oh, Malachi, yes. You feel so good inside me. Yes baby. This your pussy, Malachi. Fuck me good baby."

She cried out in complete pleasure. Kiara couldn't believe that she had finally hooked a big fish with long money and good dick. She was in pure bliss and just wanted to lay there and let him fuck her all day.

"This dick good to you baby? Huh? This dick is all yours, Kiara. Can't 'nere 'notha bitch touch this muthafucka. Yeah, baby. I'm 'bout to cum all in that pussy. Whose pussy is this? Huh baby? Tell a nigga who this pussy belongs to."

"It's yours, Malachi. This pussy is all yours! Uh yes, its yours," she yelled out and gripped the pillow tightly.

He pounded into her harder and said, "You damn right its mine and if you ever let another nigga get close to it, I'm a kill your ass. Uh shit, shit."

Malachi clenched Kiara's ass cheeks so tight that she was sure he would leave marks but she didn't care. She knew that he was deep in his zone and she would let him be. She closed her eyes as he filled her up with his seeds and wondered how he would feel if he got her pregnant. At least, she would have a child that she could tolerate because it would be by a man that cherished her. She had only known Malachi for a week but she could tell that he felt something deeper than sex with her. She deserved to be number one in a good man's life.

After Malachi emptied his nut sack into Kiara, he pulled out of her and fell back on the bed exhausted. He fucked Kiara the first night that he had met her and since she gave it up to him so fast, he knew that she would give it up to the next nigga who came along with a good story and a bank bigger than his. However, Malachi didn't like to share his pussy so he would make sure to keep Kiara on a short leash.

"Damn, Malachi, I do believe that is the best dick I've ever had and my ass been fuckin since I was fifteen."

He turned his head and looked at her and said, "Damn girl, you been giving that pussy away for a long time."

"Yeah, I know that fifteen was young but I just wanted to be loved and cherished. I thought that you had to fuck to do that," she said and then snuggled up next to him. She ran her tongue over his man nipple and cupped his flaccid dick in her hand.

"You think he can hang for another round?" She asked with a smile.

Malachi sighed and stated, "Nah baby, I think that lil nigga done for the day. Shit, you done robbed his ass of everything he had in the bank."

Kiara laughed and got up on all fours but when she started to put his dick in her mouth, he pushed her away, "Yo chill baby. This dick ain't going nowhere. Shit, save some for later."

Kiara laid back down on the bed while Malachi got up to go relieve himself. When he walked in the bathroom, he noticed Kiara's bag sitting on the counter. After he pissed and shook his dick off, he turned on the sink water and grabbed the bag. He dug through the bag and found tampons and an extra pair of thongs and other things that he expected to find in a woman's purse. He found an envelope that contained some folded up papers and took the papers out to examine them. They were paperwork to file for food stamps but as he read them he noticed something that Kiara failed to mention. He put the papers back where he got them from and then noticed something else that he didn't see before and then walked out the bathroom with rage gripping his bones.

"Damn baby, I was beginning to think that you done fell in and I was gone have to come save you," Kiara said teasingly but Malachi didn't find shit funny.

He held up the glass pipe and asked, "When the fuck you was gonna tell me you had a habit?"

Kiara looked like a deer caught in headlights and responded, "Um, I don't. That's not mine."

He threw the pipe at her and it hit the wall instead and shattered. "So, you just have a habit of walking around and carrying crack pipes for other muthafuckas. Bitch, you think I'm a dumb ass nigga or something?"

"No Malachi, I don't think that. One of my coworkers put it in there and I guess, I don't know I guess she forgot. But really, it's not mine."

Malachi nose flared in anger when he asked the next question, "Well, then I guess the child you claimed on your food stamp application ain't yours either, huh?"

"How dare you go through my shit." Kiara hollered and jumped up off the bed so she could go to the bathroom and get her bag but before she made it, Malachi grabbed a hand full of her weave and yanked her back.

"Bitch, don't you ever hide shit from me again. You want a nigga to be real with you then you need to be real back. I ain't them other muthafuckas you used to fuckin with. Do you understand me?"

Kiara tried to get out of Malachi's grip but he was too strong so she decided the best thing to do was be submissive.

"Yes, baby. I'm sorry. I'll never keep anything else from you. I just. I just didn't think you'd fuck with me if you knew I had a son. I'm sorry."

Malachi was quiet for a minute and then he asked, "Wait a minute. Your ass been up under me for almost a week now and ain't mentioned this kid. Where the fuck is your son at?"

Kiara didn't have an answer for him because she didn't know where he was. However, she knew she had to come up with something fast.

"He's at his Aunt Kaylas. He stays there a lot and I know he's in good hands. He's seventeen Malachi, so I know I don't' have to worry about him, I didn't think to mention it."

Malachi could tell she was lying but he would give her the benefit of the doubt. "Well get dressed we going take a ride to Kayla's because I would love to meet him."

Chapter 9

"Montell Banks, I hereby sentence you to seven years in the Department of Corrections. I hope you change your way of thinking and get out with a better frame of mind. You're still young son and have a whole life ahead of you. I suggest you make the best of it," The judge stated and then stood to leave the courtroom. Mellow was disappointed and shocked all at the same time because he expected to only get three to five years meaning he would have only done a little over two and got out. He was put in the police van and driven back to the county jail where he would gather his things and then be taken to the state prison, a place he had never been.

"Yo G, can I make a quick phone call so I can at least let my ole' girl know what happened?" Mellow asked the guard.

"We were advised to get you packed out and taken to the prison. You can make a phone call once you're processed," the guard replied.

"Man come on. That shit probably gonna take hours. I promise I'll be really quick."

The guard looked around to see if any other guards were around and when he saw the coast was clear, he said, "Make it quick, Banks. Say your I love yous and hang up. The transport van is waiting on you."

Mellow smiled. "Thanks man. I promise I'll be quick."

Mellow picked up the phone and dialed Big Gun's number who answered on the first ring. Big Gun pressed the number he needed to accept the call and asked, "Yo Mel, you good, dawg?"

"Big G, man them crackas gave me seven fuckin years for that shit. That fuckin lawyer told me I'd only get three to five. That shit is crazy man. The fuck I'm gonna do?"

"Damn man, I'm sorry, but you gonna take your black ass in there and do that time like a real G. A nigga got you dawg. You ain't got to worry about shit, aight man?"

"Yeah G. I hear you but damn. I know my ole girl gonna be so hurt."

"Mel, I'm a take care of your momma just like I told you. She gonna be straight man, and so are you. Don't worry about nothing."

"Come on, Banks. Hang up the phone. They're waiting on you," the guard hollered in the background.

Mellow held up a finger to let him know he was coming in one moment and then said into the phone, "Yo G, don't forget a nigga, aight. I gotta go. I love you, G." Then, he hung up.

Big Gun felt bad for his boy but he was proud of him because Mellow could have done it the pussy way out and told everything he knew but he manned up and laid it down, and for that, Mellow would be greatly rewarded.

Mellow carried his belongings to the van with shackled ankles wearing him down but he didn't complain because he had made his bed. "Yo G, you think you can take these shits off me once I step on?" He asked the guard hoping to be relieved of the cold steel.

"Nah Banks, I got to keep them on you. Policy man, sorry," the guard replied. After Mellow stepped on the van and sat down, the guard secured the caged door and then shut the doors on the transport van. An hour later, the van pulled up to the state prison and dropped Mellow off. "Take it easy Banks," the guard said and pulled away.

Mellow was taken into a strip room where he was stripped of all his clothing. He was made to spread his ass cheeks while a guard watched from behind. "Squat and cough inmate." Mellow did as the guard asked. He then showered and was given new clothes for his stay and a rule book. Then, he was escorted to his home for the next few years. Mellow walked in the small cell that had been assigned to him and shook his head. It was a far cry from what he had grown accustomed to. When he sat his bag on the bed, he heard a voice from behind him.

"Sup man? Welcome to the neighborhood."

Mellow turned around and saw two guys at his door but he was far from worried, he could hold his own if that's what they were there for. "Sup. Name's Montell but everybody calls me Mellow."

"I'm Branch. Nice to meet you. I would stay and chat but I gotta go make a call. We'll talk later," Branch said and walked away leaving his friend alone with the new cat.

"Daymion Myers. Me and Branch are your neighbors. You gonna be visiting with us long?"

Mellow looked at Daymion crazy as soon as he heard his name. He couldn't believe that he was at the same prison as the street legend himself.

"Yo dawg, it's nice to meet you but I feel like I already know you. I mean I've heard your name before but you look familiar as fuck. You sure we ain't met before?" Mellow asked.

"Nah, can't say that I know you man. What set you on?"

"I roll with Dorian Thompson. Nigga silly ass fuck though."

The name caused Daymion to reminisce. He remembered putting Dory on his first block, but Dory ended up being an ungrateful bastard. The beef got deep between them and caused a small war. Daymion had to get at Dory when he could and one day had gotten lucky and caught him off guard, but it didn't turn out as planned. As soon as Daymion popped the bullet out of the gun, Dory shifted not knowing the bullet was headed his way, and it ended up hitting Malia, Dory's pregnant girlfriend, in front of him to catch it instead. The bullet hit her in the neck and blew the main artery, never giving her or her unborn child a chance.

Mellow noticed the change in Daymion's eyes and asked, "Yo man, you aight. Did I say something wrong?"

"Nah my nigga, you good. I was just thinking about that muthafucka Dory. Who his black ass got rollin' with him now? You know I gave him his first package?" Daymion said trying to get Mellow to give him some information.

"Ah man, it's only a few of us now. It's me, my best friend Big Gun his girl's brother Teddy and a nigga they call Trap Town," Mellow said and then he remembered the other crew member and said, "Ah yeah, I almost forgot Dre. That lil nigga only eight years just starting out but his ass got dope boy potential for real. He gonna do big things in the game."

Daymion knew exactly what Dre eight year old Mellow was talking about and he was pissed but he couldn't let Mellow know just yet. He wanted to get more information out of him first so that way when he walked out the front gates in the few months, he would know exactly how to get to Dory but this time, he wouldn't miss.

***

It seemed that every time Kayla wanted to just sit back and chill, the drama came right to her front door.

"Okay, okay I'm coming," she said and opened the door only to find an unexpected visitor.

"Kiara? What the hell are you doing here? Didn't I tell you not to come back here?" She asked and looked at Kiara crazy. She wondered who the man behind her was but was for some reason afraid to ask.

Kiara said, "I just came to pick up Dre. That's all and then I'll be out and you'll never see me again."

Kayla couldn't believe what had come out of Kiara's mouth because she knew that Dre wasn't there. However, Kayla had known Kiara all her life and sensed that something was wrong so she played along.

"Um, he's not here right now. He wanted to spend the weekend with his friend, so I didn't see any harm in it. He should be back by tomorrow night though. I wish you would have called beforehand. I wouldn't have let him go."

"No, no it's okay, Kayla. However, I'd like you to meet my man, Malachi Jensen."

Kayla smiled at the stranger and got an eerie feeling in her gut. She just wanted Kiara to turn around and leave and take her new man with her, and then she remembered the money that Dre had left for his mother. "Oh, I almost forgot. Dre left me something to give to you. Why don't you follow me to my room, and I'll get it for you. Malachi, why don't you make yourself comfortable?"

"Yeah, I'll do that but hurry up. We got shit to do," Malachi said as the two women took off to the bedroom. Once the door was shut behind them, Kayla lit into Kiara. "What the fuck do you really want Kiara? You knew that Dre wasn't here so why did you lie to that man, and bring him to my place?"

"I'm sorry, Kayla but I didn't know what else to do. I've been with him the past few days and forgot to mention that I had a son. When he found out, he was pissed because he don't want no secrets between us. I couldn't let him know that I didn't know where my child is. For God's sake, he is not an adult yet and I just left him to fend for himself. How do you think Malachi would feel about me then?"

"He's seventeen now, Kiara. He just had a birthday and I haven't seen him since. He came by long enough to drop some money off for you. He's out there selling drugs in the fucking streets, Kiara but all your worried about is a man you just met. Take this damn money and get the hell out before I tell your new man the truth."

Kiara snatched the wad of bills out of Kayla's hand and said, "Fuck you, Kayla. If you see my son again, call me immediately." Then, she opened the room door to leave only to see Malachi staring back at her.

***

Dre peeked through the bushes and watched his momma and some man he had never seen before knock on his Auntie Kayla's door. Something in his gut told him to remain where he was even though Although, he wanted to go see what the hell was going on.

He was angry at his momma because she hadn't been out looking for him. He knew that she hated him but she didn't have to be so cruel. He wondered how she would feel when Kayla gave her the money he left behind. He hoped that it would enough to help her with some of the bills. It was all he had left over from buying some more clothes and shoes. Thanks to Shay stealing money from Dory's pot, he was able to keep some extra cash.

He even ran into the nice lady that paid for his first new outfit. There was no way he would ever forget her. He was proud of himself for returning the money the lady had loaned him. He saw her at the same Goodwill. He just happened to be passing by and noticed her at the counter. Dre then walked into the store and when he did, he heard the same cashier from behind the counter.

"Oh no. It's you again. You better have enough money in your little pockets this time because ain't nobody paying your bill. You hear me?"

Dre ignored her and walked up to the lady he had been looking for. "Excuse me. Do you remember me?" He asked.

The lady took a minute and then remembered. "Oh my Gosh. I do remember you. How could I forget such a handsome young man? Are you okay? Do you need me to help you pay for something?"

"No ma'am. I'm only here to give you your money back just like I promised," Dre said and handed the lady a fifty-dollar bill.

She tried to give it back to him and said, "Oh no, son, I did that out of the kindness of my heart not because I wanted it back. Besides, it's too much."

Dre refused to take the money back, "It's okay. You keep it anyway. I was just trying to keep my word. Have a good day."

She smiled and said, "Thank you, son. You are going to grow up and be a wonderful man."

Dre turned and when he walked past the cashier he waved and said, "I don't need anything in here anymore, so you won't see me again. Besides, your stuff is too cheap anyway."

The sound of hollering broke Dre from his thoughts and looked back toward the apartment complex. The man that his mother was with pushed her against his jeep and hollered, "Bitch, didn't I tell you not to tell me anymore lies? The fuck you think you playing with? Now get your ass in. I'll deal with you when we get home."

"Home," Dre said to himself, but wasn't sure what the man meant. Dre waited until the jeep drove away and then came out of the bushes. He rushed up the stairs that led to the apartment he lived in with his mother but when he got there, the door was locked. He looked under the welcome mat for the extra key, but it was gone. He swore he heard voices coming from the other side of the door, so he knocked. When the door opened, it was a man that he hadn't been familiar with. The man asked, "What's up? Who you looking for?"

Dre asked, "Who are you and why you in my momma's apartment?"

"Your momma. I don't know who your momma is but me and my wife moved in here two days ago. I'm sorry. Do you need me to call somebody?"

Dre held his head low so the man wouldn't see his tears. "No thanks." and walked away. He walked up to the next floor and knocked on Kayla's door hoping that he at least still had her.

***

Shay still lay in the same position that Dory had left her in, but he wasn't going to let her ruin his night with the fine young red bone he had just met.

"Don't mind that bitch, baby. Just go ahead and take that shit off. A nigga ready to smell that pussy," Dory said as he undressed.

The girl heard Shay whimper and hesitated, but Dory brought her there to fuck not to be sympathetic.

"Yo, you gonna worry about that thieving bitch or you gonna worry about this dick? Take that shit off or get the hell out."

She slowly began to undress and tried to forget about the woman lying in a pool of blood on the floor. She asked, "Who is that, Dory?"

"Bitch, it's about to be you if you don't get naked. Come on now, a nigga nuts is full. Come suck this muthfucka and empty these bitches."

Dory stroked his hardened dick and watched the woman get naked. His precum oozed out of the tip when he saw her shaved pussy. "Damn baby, that shit fat as fuck."

She smiled at Dory's comment. She had been trying to cuff Dory for a minute, but he just never seemed to notice her. She didn't want to do anything to ruin the night that lay ahead of her, so she pushed the images of the woman out of her mind and pulled Dory's dick between her lips. He put a hand on the back of her head and pushed her head down until she almost choked. Dory knew that God had blessed him, and he always used it to his advantage. What more could any woman want than money and a man with a big dick.

"Yeah, baby just like that," He said as her head bobbed up and down.

She liked the fact that she was making him feel good, but she was ready to feel good too. She released him from her mouth and asked, "Damn Dory, when you gonna get in this pussy and make me feel good?"

"Shit, sucking this big muthafucka should a made you feel good but I understand so come on and wet this dick up."

She smiled and stood up over him straddling his waist. She came down until the tip of his dick was at her opening but as soon as his head was inside of her, she heard someone call out to Dory.

"Dory. Yo, nigga where you at?" Big Gun hollered out.

Dory hollered back, "I'm back here getting serviced nigga. Come on and join me."

Big Gun walked in the room and saw the redbone make Dory's dick disappear inside of her. She pulled on her hardened nipples and look into Big Gun's eyes and said, "You came right on time."

Big Gun shook his head and turned to walk out of the room but out of the corner of his eyes he saw someone else. "The fuck," he asked and ran to Shay as she laid on the floor. "Yo D. Man, what the fuck is wrong with you?"

"Man, fuck that bitch. Her ass has been the one stealing from me. I caught her with her hand in the pot. Let that bitch stay there and die. Stupid bitch."

Big Gun made sure that Shay was still alive and then went to the bathroom and got a bath robe to cover her in. "Nigga,

I knew you was foul as fuck but this shit is uncalled for. Teddy gonna be pissed."

"Man, fuck Teddy. That fat nigga can get it too. Keep riding this dick, baby don't worry about what else is goin on. You bout to make me cum, and when you do I'm a reward you real good."

"I'm outta here. I got to get Shay to the hospital." Big Gun said as he pulled Shay into his arms so he could carry her to his truck. Before he walked out, he turned to look at Dory one more time and wondered how he could fuck another bitch as Shay laid there bleeding out. He shook his head in disappointment because he knew that the crew would never be the same after that this.

Chapter 10

Teddy got to the hospital as quickly as he could and as soon as he walked in, he saw Big Gun pacing the floor and ran up to him. "Yo, I got here as fast as I could. What the fuck is going on with my sister?"

"Teddy, I'm gonna let Shay tell you exactly what happened but promise me you won't show your ass. You gonna have to chill on this."

"The fuck you mean, chill? Man, whoever did that foul shit to my sister is gonna pay."

Big Gun wanted Teddy to calm down so he could go see about Shay. He already knew what was going to happen once Teddy found out that it was Dory that put her there and he also knew there was no way he could prevent it.

"Hey just go in the room and check on your sister, dawg. She needs you right now so don't worry about who did it. We'll take care of that later."

"Yeah, aight G, you right. I got to focus on Shay," Teddy said and walked into the room where she was being held at. His heart broke as soon as he saw her. He was mad at himself because he was supposed to protect her from all of the coldness and evil of the world. He was really all she had, and he had let her down. How would he go to the rehabilitation center and tell their grandfather that Shay was laid up in a hospital bed bruised and beaten and that she wouldn't be making it on Sunday to cook him dinner? He knew that the news would cause him to go deeper into his web of depression and that worried him even more.

He looked at Shay's swollen face and tears formed in his eyes. Who could have done such a horrible thing to a person as wonderful as her? He then wondered where Dory was and why he wasn't there. Teddy heard the door open behind him and looked to see Big Gun come inside.

"How's she doing Teddy?" Big Gun asked in a concerned voice.

"I 'ont know man. I ain't been able to ask nobody and she won't wake up to tell me nothing."

"Yeah, she lost a lot of blood on the way here but other than that, I think she's gonna be fine. I'm a go find the nurse and try to get some information aight," Big Gun started to leave, but Teddy's next question stopped him in his tracks.

"Yo G, why Dory ass ain't here?"

Big Gun didn't answer but instead gave him a look that he read very well.

"I'm a kill that muthafucka." Teddy rushed the door, but Big Gun jumped in front of him "Nah, dawg, we'll handle that shit later. You need to stay your big ass here and take care of her. She's all you need to worry about. Okay?"

Teddy breathed heavily with a look of death in his eyes "Yeah, you right but that nigga gonna see me. Foul ass bastard." He then turned around and went back to Shay's side so he could wait for her to wake up and find out what really went down. He had a feeling and if it was right, he'd be coming for him too but he wouldn't give Dory a chance because he would go to him first.

***

Dre knocked on Kayla's door with a purpose. He wanted some answers, and he wasn't leaving until he got some.

When Kayla opened the door for him, she smiled and pulled him into her "Oh Dre, baby I'm so happy to see you, but where the hell have you been? Your father been asking about you."

He wasn't there for sentiments, though. "Why you ain't tell me my momma moved out?"

Kayla hesitated at first but ultimately answered him "Dre, I didn't know until she showed up here with her new man looking for you. She wanted me to lie and tell Malachi that you had been staying with me. I played it off so they would leave."

"Why does that chump care where I'm staying? He 'ont even know me."

"She's trying to make herself out to sound like a good mother I'm guessing. She wants to paint a perfect picture so Malachi will want to stay with her."

"And you lied for her?"

"I didn't actually lie. I just didn't tell everything I knew. Look Dre, I don't know why you're out there in them streets, but you know that you can stay here with me for as long as you like."

"Yeah, you only saying that because you trying to get in good with my daddy."

"No Dre, I mean it. You know how much you mean to me regardless; besides, we still have to celebrate you turning nine seventeen, Big Man," Kayla said and pulled Dre into her arms but he wasn't buying her charade. At one time, he could feel the love that Kayla had for him but now he wasn't so sure. He hadn't been sure of anything anymore.

He pulled back from her embrace "I got somewhere to be, but I'll be back."

Kayla looked at him disappointedly and knew that she should force him to stay but she vowed that she would never make him do things that he didn't want to do. "Okay, but let me give you something before you go," Kayla went to her bag and pulled out a set of keys. She took one off the key ring and handed it to him "Use this whenever you need it, no matter what time of day or night. Okay?"

Dre took the key and put it in his pocket and smiled a half smile. "Thanks, Auntie Kayla. I'll be back." Then, he turned around and walked out to go to his next destination.

***

Dory barely heard the knock on his door and at first, thought he was hearing things and went back to what he was doing, but the knock came again. He pulled his piece out and checked the clip to make sure that he was ready just in case it was someone with some drama. He hadn't been expecting anybody but after the beating he put on Shay, he was sure that Teddy would be paying him a visit really soon, but he had something for Teddy's ass too.

Before he made it to the door, the knock came again. Dory peeked through a small space in the window blinds and saw Dre standing at his door. He put his gun down in the waist of his jeans and unlatched the door.

"Sup, lil nigga? I hope you here to pay me my shit back."

Dre was confused because he didn't know what Dory was talking about. He asked, "What you mean, pay you back? I'm here to give you what I made off that last pack."

Dory grabbed the front of Dre's shirt and yanked him further into the room "Lil nigga, you think I'm stupid or something? You ain't think I was gonna find out who been stealing out of my pot? Huh?"

A feeling of fear filled Dre, but it wasn't himself that he was concerned with. "Where Shay at?" He asked fearfully.

"That bitch is where she needs to be at. You thought I was gonna let her keep stealing from me. That bitch had me looking at my boys crazy and shit like they done turned on me and the whole time it was her ass. Stealing for your punk ass. The fuck you and my bitch got going on?"

Dre stayed quiet and his heart felt as if it would beat out of his chest. He would never sell Shay out, he would rather die.

Dory continued, "Tell me, Lil Spade. Where the hell you been getting the money from to pay me?"

Dre hesitated but knew that he had to answer the question. "I been out there on my block where you put me. Them fiends done got used to me so they come look for me before anybody else."

The push came so fast, Dre couldn't stop it and he was on the floor in no time. He knew he shoulda got himself a gun.

"So you gonna stand here and lie to my face? Do you think I give a fuck about how old you are? Nigga, you came to me for work, and I put you on and yet, you gonna take money that my bitch stole from me to pay me. Huh! You know, y'all muthafuckas had me going for a minute but the party is over," Dory stated and pulled out his gun. He pointed it at Dre who now had tears in his eyes, "Oh no, you gonna act like a little bitch. Huh? You asked to lead a dope boy lifestyle, and this here is just part of the game."

Dre tried to save him. "Please Dory. Man, I'll work double. I'll work, day and night but don't kill me. I'll get back out on the block right now."

"Oh, you begging? You a pussy just like your fuckin' daddy. That muthafucka took my seed and now it's time I pay him back."

Dre squeezed his eyes shut and prayed as hard as he could. His life hadn't been the greatest, but he wasn't ready to die. He had just turned seventeen and wanted to be here when his pops came home in a few months. nThey had so much to catch up on. He was just trying to make his momma proud, but he never expected it to be this way. He sat and waited for a shot that never came because the sound of the front door being kicked in stopped Dory from pulling the trigger back.

Dre heard Teddy's voice and opened his eyes. "You fucking bastard! How dare you put your hands on my sister. Nigga, you was supposed to take care of her, not hurt her, what's up with that?" Teddy said as he looked Dory in the eyes.

"Oh yeah, you here to straighten some shit that your sister did. Nigga you call yourself checkin' me? That bitch deserved it. The fuck she thought? I had my fingers pointed at y'all muthafuckas but it was her the entire time. And all for this lil' bastard. The fuck up with that Teddy?"

"She was protecting him from Malice who you kept sending out there to rob him. That was some foul shit, Dory."

"Ah, I was just trying to toughen the lil nigga up. That's all. How his ass gonna play in the big leagues and act like he on a little league field. Nigga, this shit ain't softball. That games for pussies. Muthafucka was supposed to man up and fight back."

"It still gives you no right to put your hands on Shay. Now put your piece up and let's handle this like two grown men."

"Oh, you call yourself coming up in my shit to fight me 'bout a replaceable bitch."

"Muthafucka that's my sister and family is off limits you know the rules."

"Yeah, that's your sister but that was my bitch. She was sucking this dick every night but that didn't give her the right to steal my shit and every time I see her, I'm a beat that bitch ass, and your fat ass ain't gonna do shit about it."

Teddy landed the punch before Dory could move out of the way and blood flew from Dory's lips and sprayed on to Dre's T-shirt. Dre jumped up from the floor and backed up against a wall. He wished that there was something he could do to stop them because his heart told him how things would end up. He felt like shit because none of this would have happened if he would have stayed his ass at home. He wanted to please his momma so bad that he would have done anything. Although, he knew deep down nothing would make her love him.

"Bitch, you should have never put your hands on my fucking sister. You muthafucka. She ain't deserve that shit!" Teddy hollered and with every word landed punches. Blood covered Dory's face and Teddy was too big for Dory to fight back. His only line of defense would be his weapon which was now across the floor after being knocked out of his hand.

Something in Dre's mind told him to go pick up the weapon but he was too afraid to move. Finally, Teddy stopped the blows to Dory's swollen and bloodied face. He got up off of Dory and said, "Nigga, I came here with the intent to murder your ass but you ain't even worth a fuckin bullet. Don't ever let me catch you around my fuckin sister again anymore because if I have to come here again on some bullshit, I won't hesitate."

Teddy looked at Dre "Let's go, Lil Spade. You free from that nigga now."

Dre opened the front door with Teddy behind him so they could leave with no intentions of ever coming back. As soon as Dre stepped out the front door, a shot rang out. Dre heard a loud thud but was afraid to turn his head and look behind him. Somehow, he already knew what he would find. However, his curiosity got the better of him so he turned and looked hoping that he would see Teddy still there. A tear had already formed in the well of his eyes, but he refused to give in and let it win. He looked and saw Teddy, but he was no longer behind him, protecting him from the evil that had unknowingly loomed over him. Instead, he looked right into Dory's face that now held a wicked smile. Teddy lay in front of him on the floor with a bullet hole in the back of his head.

Dory said, "Nigga, should have handled his business. Now, get out there and make my fucking money."

***

The bright lights of the strip club seemed to illuminate the entire sky. Dre had never been there before although, he was familiar with the establishment. It was where his mother worked but Dre didn't know that she had stopped dancing there. It was all that she talked about when she brought men home at night. No one seemed to notice him in the cut because they were all in their own world. The men came there to see women dance and take their clothes off so he was the last thing on their dirty minds.

Dre watched until there was no one else in the parking lot and yet, he still hadn't saw his mother. He wondered if she was off or something. It broke his heart to know that she hadn't even been worried about him and then he wondered if she ever would.

He decided to leave the club and go back to Kayla's. He knew that he couldn't return to Dory's because the sight of Teddy lying on the floor with a bullet in his head would play over and over again. Dre was halfway down the block when a car pulled up beside him. "Hey, ain't it kinda late for you to be out?"

Dre looked to the man who asked him that question and responded, "What is it to you?"

"Oh, okay I see I'm bothering you. My bad."

The man looked familiar to Dre, but he couldn't quite place him and Dre didn't know if he should run or chill.

"You need a ride somewhere?" The man asked.

Dre thought about it for a minute and knew that he should never get in a stranger's car. He looked at the man really good and then remembered where he had saw him at. "Aye, ain't you that man that's been hanging out with my momma?"

The man replied, "That depends on who your momma is."

"My momma's Kiara Taylor."

Malachi smiled at him, he just couldn't believe his luck. "Oh shit, you must be Dreighton. I've heard a lot about you." The lie was so easy for him to tell. The truth was that Kiara hardly ever mentioned Dre, but he wanted the kid to feel comfortable.

"My name's Dre and I'm sure she ain't had nothing good to say. She's never said anything good," Dre said in a sad voice.

"Actually, she only talks good about you. She's been going crazy with worry not knowing where you been."

"Yeah. She probably glad I'm not around."

"Nah, kid. Your momma loves you. Maybe she just doesn't know how to show it. Come on and get in and I'll take you to her."

Dre thought about it for a minute and wasn't sure if he should trust Malachi, but it was either get in the car and go to where his mother was or walk to Kayla's and risk getting seen by Dory or maybe even Malice. He couldn't depend on Teddy to save him anymore because he was dead. Against Dre's better judgement he opened the door and got in "Alright, but you gotta take my straight to my momma."

"Ah kid, you safe with me. I just got one stop to make before we go."

"Yeah. Aight."

Chapter 11

"Hey Tasha, where Kendrick at?" Malice asked when he walked up in the yard. Tasha was Kendrick's fifiteen year-old sister and his most prized possession.

"Do I look like I keep up with him?" She asked and continued to hang the clothes she had just washed on the line.

Malice knew that Kendrick and Tasha's grandma was pulling a double shift at the hospital so she wouldn't be home until later. He also knew that Kendrick had left ten minutes before he got there because he watched him leave. He knew that this would be the perfect opportunity to pay Kendrick back for jumping on him.

He stepped a little closer to Tasha and asked, "What's up, Tasha? You know a nigga been feeling you for a minute now. I say we get into a little something while we are alone."

Tasha stopped what she was doing and turned to him. She put her hands on her hips and said with an attitude, "Well, I say you have done lost your damn mind. I'm saving myself for the man I'm gonna marry and I don't see that man being you."

"Oh yeah, well how you know I ain't the one you gonna marry? That's real foul. Shit, I could see myself spending forever with a chick like you."

Tasha blushed at his comment, but she wasn't naïve and wasn't buying what he was selling. "Pst, when you put a ring on this finger and walk me down the aisle, I'll let you tear it up but until then, you gonna wait."

"Well, then I guess you got a problem."

Tasha turned and bent over to pick up a sheet out of the laundry basket so that she could hang it up with the rest of the laundry and when she did, Malice pushed her to the ground. She fell face first into the freshly cut grass.

"Damn Malice, what the hell you do that for?" She asked and started to get up, but Malice had other plans. He pushed her back down and started to undo his jeans. When she tried to get up again, he kicked her in the ribcage. "Stay your ass down, bitch."

Tasha began to cry because she didn't know what was happening or even why it was. She had never been anything but nice to Malice for as long as she could remember.

"Ow Malice, what was that for?" She asked and held her side. She turned her head so she could see what he was doing and saw him pull out his dick. He stood in front of her and then dropped to his knees and said, "That was for your fuck ass brother. Now come here and put me in your mouth."

Malice grabbed a handful of Tasha's freshly braided weave while she slung her fists and tried to fight him off, but he was too strong.

"Stop it Malice. Please you're hurting me."

"Come here and put it in your mouth then."

No matter how hard he tried, Tasha would not open her mouth, so he said, "Aight then, you wanna be stubborn. I'll put this muthafucka somewhere else."

When Malice let go of her hair, she tried to get up again and he kicked her in the ribs making her lose her breath. He then grabbed the waist of her shorts and yanked them down. "You shoulda just sucked it and I woulda spared your ass."

"No, please Malice, please I'll suck it, I swear but please don't do this." Tasha begged while the pain of his kick soared through her body. "Please. Please I'll do it." Malice had kicked her so hard she swore that one or more of her ribs was broken. She was in so much pain that she could no longer fight.

When Malice had her shorts and panties all the way off, he got behind her, spread her open and said, "That's right Tasha, beg bitch." Then, he pushed himself inside of her.

***

Daymion liked Mellow's style and knew that he was a nigga he could fuck with on the outside, but he would have to get him out of Dory's grasp. Mellow was still young but he seemed to be good people. Day vowed to keep it real and hold him down once he got out because Mellow would still have a few years left on the inside when Day bounced.

"So, you say that Dory got a little nigga called Dre down with his team?" Day asked Mellow while they chilled on the bench and watched the other inmates shoot a game of basketball. Daymion lit a joint and passed it to Mellow.

"Yeah man, the little nigga just popped up one day and asked my man to put him on. He said he wanted to help his momma out and make a little bread to help pay bills."

True enough, Daymion had been Dre's age when he started in the game, but he had someone he looked up to guiding him. Someone he knew that he was safe with. Day knew that Dory had to know that Dre was his son and felt like Dory was only using it as bait. A way to pay him back for what he'd done years before.

He thought back to the night that he accidentally killed Malia. The chick that Dory had been caking it up with who just happened to be pregnant at the time. Their beef had started about eight months after Daymion put Dory on.

"That's how you gonna act after a nigga puts you on huh?" Daymion asked Dory one night on the block he had given him to control.

"Yeah man, that's how I'm gonna act. I'm taking this block over and you just gonna have to accept it. I got too much potential to keep working under a mufucka. I need to do my own thang."

"Sounds like you done got too big for your fuckin drawers. Maybe I need to bring your ass back down to size nigga. This my shit out here and if you would a stepped to me like a real muthafucka, I might have made a compromise but bitch you work for me, not the other way around," Daymion said arguing while he got up in Dory's face.

"Yeah, well I quit and now I'm gonna do my own thing and I'm gonna do it on this block. Whether you accept it or not."

"Aight playa, I see how you doing it and you know what, I'm gonna give you a week to think about what you doing. I'm coming back and I hope by then you done came to your senses. If not, I'm bringing your ass that heat," Daymion said and walked away. He didn't want to resort to gunplay but he'd be damned if he allowed Dory to disrespect him and the rest of his crew.

The next night, Dory had some goons run up in one of Daymion's houses and rob them. Day waited a couple of days until he thought Dory was comfortable and then saw him outside of a Kentucky Fried Chicken. He had his bitch Malia with him, and Daymion happened to drive by while he was opening the door for her. Dory turned his head just in time to see Day pop his gat and moved out of the way but it put Malia in full view. The bullet struck her in the neck and before she could be helped, she bled out. Now, Daymion and Dory had an even deeper beef.

Mellow pulled on the joint and passed it back to Daymion, who took it and inhaled as much smoke as he could. He wasn't going to tell Mellow about the beef between him and Dory because he would need him to tell where Dory laid his head. However, Daymion had another beef out there, one that he had no clue about and as soon as he was a free man, that beef would be coming to his front door.

***

Malachi pulled up to a two-story house condo and parked his ride. He looked over at Dre in his passenger seat and said, "Get out lil nigga, I got to run up in here real quick and then we going to where your momma at."

Dre looked at him sleepily. "Nah, I'm tired. Can I just sit out here and wait for you?"

"Nah, you gonna bring your ass in so I can keep an eye on you. Now, get out and come on," Malachi hollered.

Dre let out a long sigh and did what he said. He wondered why they were even there. If his momma wasn't in that house, then who was? Malachi pulled out a key and unlocked the door. He looked at Dre and told him, "Go on in. I don't trust your little ass, and don't touch nothing in there."

Malachi walked in behind him and when he shut the door, he hollered out, "Yo Bree, bring that ass down the stairs. A nigga needs a real meal."

Dre wondered who Bree was and then heard someone coming down the stairs. He looked and saw a half-naked woman walk down with a smile on her face.

"Well, it's about damn time you show up. Where's that bitch at?"

"Don't worry about her. You just worry about this big muthafucka in front of you," Malachi said and put her hand on his dick. Bree suddenly noticed that they were not alone. "Uh, who the hell is that?"

"Oh, that's Dre. I'm just giving him a ride to his momma's but a nigga decided to take a detour. I couldn't go no longer without a fix, so what's up?"

She laughed and said, "You know I got you baby but what about him? What's he gonna do while I take care of you?"

"He gonna sit his ass right there and wait for me to get done. .Now, come on and take that shit off. Let me admire that package you carrying."

"Mmm, I think I can do that."

Bree then took off the small tank top that barely covered her perky breasts. Malachi turned to Dre and asked, "You ever seen such pretty ass titties? Huh lil nigga?"

Dre turned his head, but Malachi wanted him to pay attention.

"Nigga turn your head back and watch. I know you ain't scared of some pussy. You probably done watched that whore you call a momma a dozen times so don't act all shy and shit now."

Dre turned his head back and when he did, Malachi grabbed a hold of Bree's thongs and pulled them down. "Baby, I don't feel comfortable doing this in front of him can we go upstairs to the room please."

"Nah, that nigga been out in them streets doing big men things so his ass ready for shit like this."

"Well, shouldn't his daddy be teaching him stuff like this instead?" She asked.

Malachi replied, "His daddy? That muthafucka been in prison since the day this lil nigga was born. If he waits on his daddy, he ain't gon' never learn shit. Now come on."

"Uh-Uh. Malachi. I ain't about to let you disrespect me like that. Come on and let's go to the room. I'm a make it well worth it."

"Damn Bree, you better be glad I'm horny as a mufucka and you better ride this dick good." He wondered if his momma knew about the woman and what purpose she served in Malachi's life. Dre now wished that he would have gone to Kayla's like he started to do. He just wasn't sure about Kayla anymore, though. He had been let down so much and felt like she would let him down too and he just didn't want to give her that chance.

"Yeah baby, ride it like you mean it."

Dre tried to ignore the sounds coming from up the stairs, but it was very hard. He began to think about Shay and imagined her riding his manhood one-day the same way that Bree was riding Malachi. He may have only been seventeen years old, but he knew what he wanted. He only hoped that Shay would want the same thing. He was so deep in thought that he didn't realize the couple had finished their act and came back down in the living room.

"Aye yo, nigga where the hell your mind at? I said let's go," Malachi said and broke Dre from his thoughts. He looked at Malachi and saw him chewing as if he had just got done eating. It reminded Dre that he hadn't ate anything and it caused his stomach to growl.

Bree asked, "You think I should fix him a plate. It sounds like he's hungry."

"Hell nah, you ain't his momma. Let that bitch feed him," Malachi said and guzzled down his beer to wash the food down. He bent down and kissed Bree and then said, "Come on. I'm a take you to your momma and you better not say shit about anything you've seen, or I'm a make your ass regret it."

***

Kayla had fallen asleep on the couch while she waited for Dre to show up so when she woke up, it was no surprise that her whole body ached. However, her concern was fixed solely on the kid little boy who felt that no one cared about him. Kayla got up and looked around her apartment so she could check for any signs that Dre had been there, but she found nothing. She finally decided that she would get herself together and then go look for him. She felt like she knew exactly where to start.

She took a shower and brushed her teeth and then got dressed in jeans that showed a figure fit for a black woman. She was always amazed at how her body transformed from a flat ass and no breasts to something only a plastic surgeon could have put together. The only difference was Kayla's body was natural and she embraced every inch of it along with all the men she'd ever been with. She hoped that one day Daymion Myers would have control of it because she felt like he would cherish it.

"Alright Dre, please be where I can find you," she said to herself when she started her car. She decided to go to the area that she heard Dre hung around in. It was an area other white girls would have been nervous about but not Kayla. She was a thoroughbred and felt comfortable with the black race. They were more like family to her than any of the white people she'd encountered.

When Kayla got to the block, she drove slowly in hopes of seeing him, but she had no luck. She finally parked at a store and got out to ask a few people if they'd seen him, but no one seemed to know who she was talking about. She decided that she would go on back home and pray that he showed up. How would she break the news to Daymion?

"Yo, Snow, what's up Shawty? What you out here looking for?"

Kayla heard the man behind her ask but wasn't sure if he was talking to her so she turned around. "Are you talking to me?"

Trap Town looked her up and down and replied to her question. "Well, you seem to be the only snowflake around. You need something?"

"Uh no, I'm not out here looking for drugs. I'm looking for my nephew."

"Aight, my bad, shawty. Maybe I can help you out."

Kayla pulled out her phone and showed Trap Town the picture she had of Dre on it.

As soon as he saw it, he said, "Yeah, I might have seen that lil nigga around but what's in it for me?"

She replied, "A clear conscience, that's what. He just turned seventeen years old and has no business out here. I just want to make sure that he's okay. Please tell me where to find him."

Trap Town wasn't as cold hearted as people thought he was, and he could see the genuine concern in the woman's eyes. He finally let his compassion get the better of him and said, "That lil nigga works for Dory but I'm telling you now, Dory ain't gonna let him go that easy, but you can try." He told here where to go, and Kayla immediately jumped in her car to follow his directions. Before she pulled off, he hollered out. "Hey Snow, don't tell him I sent you and good luck."

Kayla pulled up the house that Trap Town sent her to and when she got out of the car, chills ran the length of her spine. But her chills weren't from fear, they were from the anticipation of hopefully seeing Dre. She looked around at the dealers trying to catch the early morning fiends. A lone patrol car slowly passed by at the top of the block somehow knowing not to stop. This was how a lot of these men paid their bills and kept food on their tables. The job force wasn't very nice to the black man, so they did what they needed to do in order to provide for their families. The officers that patrolled the area respected that as long as no gun violence occurred. When that happened, that is when they would step in.

Kayla walked up on the porch of the house very slowly because she wasn't sure of what to expect. She could have sworn that someone was watching her but still played it cool. She had to think about Dre and nothing else because he was the one that mattered. She lifted her hand and formed a small fist so that she could knock on the door but before her flesh touched the wood, a voice came from behind her.

"Who the hell are you, white girl?" Dory asked while he admired the curves of the woman who had her back to him.

Kayla turned around and looked Dory in the eyes. "I'm, I'm Kayla. I'm looking for my nephew."

"Ain't no white kids up in there so you looking in the wrong place."

"No, um. No, my nephew's not white. He's a black kid. His name is Dreighton and I got a picture of him if you'd like to see it." Kayla pulled out her phone but before she had a chance to show Dory the picture, he snatched the phone out of her hand.

Kayla put on a brave face. Although, her heart was about to beat out of her chest. He looked at the phone and smiled at Kayla.

"Yeah, I know that nigga. Matter of fact, I been looking for him too."

"What you mean by you been looking for him too? You're not gonna hurt him, are you?"

"Hell no, that's my lil nigga. He wanted to make some bread so he could help his momma out or something like that, so I gave him a lil help, but I ain't seen him in a few days." Dory lied. He liked what he saw in front of him and didn't want to seem so hard. He then asked, "Hey, you want to come in and get something to drink? Maybe we could go out together and see if we can find him."

Kayla knew she should have said no because the man in front of her gave her a queasy feeling deep in her gut but her main concern was Dre and it might have been her only chance to find him. "Well, I guess I could use something to drink." She smiled and when Dory opened the door, she walked in behind him.

***

122

The day for Shay to get released from the hospital had finally come. Teddy was supposed to pick her up and she had everything ready to go so when he got there, they could just leave. She had gotten tired of laying in that bed and the longer she was there, the more she thought about the baby that Dory had beaten out of her. She wanted to keep her baby but maybe it was best that she had no ties to Dorian Thompson anymore. She would finally be able to entertain her feelings for Dre and she couldn't wait.

She heard the door open and saw that it was Big Gun instead of Teddy and became confused. "Where's my brother at? He said he was coming to get me when it was time."

"Uh yeah. Um, he had every intention to Shay but he's not gonna be able to make it."

"Why do you look like you have more to tell me than that? Where the hell is my brother, Big Gun and where is Dre?"

"Yo, I think I should just get you outta here now and we'll talk about everything else in the car."

Shay could feel that something was wrong, but he didn't want to tell her. However, she wasn't taking one step out of that hospital until he did. "I'm not going anywhere until you tell me where Teddy is at."

"He's dead, Shay. Teddy's gone."

Shay felt like she was going to be sick to her stomach. She fell to the floor and put her face in her hands. "No, you're lying, Gun. Your fucking lying to me. Tell me where the hell he is and stop playing."

Big Gun bent down beside Shay and stated, "I'm sorry, I wish that I was playing but I'm not. He went to Dory's to pay him back for what he done to you and things didn't turn out so good for him. Dory shot him in the back of the head when he tried to leave. Dre was there with him."

"No. No. No. Not Teddy. He was a good dude. He wasn't cold hearted like him. No. How am I gonna go on without him? He was all I had left." Shay cried out as Gun pulled her into his arms. He hated to be the bearer of bad news but who else was there to give it to her uncut.

Dory had divided the crew because now things would never be the same between them. He knew that the division would weaken the organization, but he would try to stand tall and keep shit together. Dory had killed one of their own and there was no excuse for it.

Big Gun and Teddy had been friends for as long as he could remember, and Shay was like his little sister. They all had come from good families and were raised to do the right thing. Although, Teddy and him had listened to the streets when they called for them. Teddy had been the one that got in Dory's crew first and then recruited Gun. Trap and Mellow came in after them. They had all formed a brotherly bond from the beginning but somewhere along the ride, Dory changed routes.

Teddy has introduced Shay to Dory against his will because when she first met him, she had to have him. All Teddy wanted was for his baby sister to be happy. He truly thought that by Shay being family Dory would do right by her but instead, he always had other women even if she was around. He held no respect for her but somewhere deep inside, Shay had love for him and only wanted to make it work. The more Big Gun thought about it, the angrier he became. He decided that he was going to have to pull back from Dory. Although, he knew it wasn't going to be easy. He could start his own thing because he knew the connect personally and now regretted ever hooking him up with Dory.

He loosened his hold around Shay and said, "Come on, sis. I'm gonna take you home. We got to make some arrangements to bury Teddy."

"Oh, Gun, how am I gonna go on without him? He was my everything."

"I know it's gonna be hard but we can do it. That was my boy. He was like a brother to me and I give you my word, Dory is gonna pay for taking him from us but right now, we gotta focus on other things. You think Teddy would want to see us here like this? Hell nah, that nigga would want us to spark one and smoke it in his memory," Gun said and brought a smile to Shay's face. He knew that since Teddy was gone, he was going to have to step up to the plate and be her source of strength. He vowed to have her back at all costs.

"Come on, Shay, let's get outta here," he said and stood up. He reached a hand out to her and she took it so he could pull her up. She was glad to have someone in her life like Big Gun because without him, she would have completely broke.

The hospital room door opened, and a nurse walked in with a wheelchair and said, "Here's your ride downstairs."

Shay looked at the nurse crazy and stated, "Uh, nah I think I'll pass. I'm sure I can make it down without one."

"Sorry ma'am, hospital policy. It's just a precaution. You have to roll up outta here in this or you don't leave."

Shay looked for Gun to help but he just shrugged and then went and took control of the wheelchair.

"Come on, Shay. Afterall, it is policy."

Shay let out a loud sigh and then sat in the chair so Gun could push her. She was ready to get out of there so she could go live her life free of Dorian Thompson. She just hoped that he would let her.

Chapter 12

"Where that blood come from?" Malachi asked Dre after he noticed the small drops of splatter on his shirt. Dre had forgotten all about the blood that flew on him from Dory when Teddy punched him. Malachi asked him that question and it made him think about the bullet that ended Teddy's life.

"Hey lil nigga, you hear me talking to you?" Malachi asked out of frustration. "Where the hell that blood come from? I don't see your ass bleeding from anywhere so that must mean it belongs to someone else."

"It doesn't matter where it came from. That ain't your damn business."

"Oh, I see you got a flip ass mouth just like your momma. Don't make me check your ass because you ain't gonna like it. Now answer my fuckin question."

"There was a fight and some of the blood spattered. That's all."

"Yeah, I'll let you have that for now but you gonna learn some manners fuckin with me."

Dre's heart began to beat faster. He wished that he'd never gotten in that car with Malachi. All he wanted to do was see what was up with his momma and then he'd be on his way.

"Aight. We here. Get your ass out and remember what the hell I said. Don't say shit about where we just came from."

"Was that your girlfriend?"

Malachi snickered but answered the question. "Yeah that was my bitch. She been holding a nigga down for a minute now. You'll find you one like that one day."

"Then, what you doing with my momma? And you don't know if I ain't already got one like that?"

"Yeah you might have one but when it comes to your momma, the fuck is it to you? I'm tearing that pussy up. That's what the fuck I'm doing. You got a problem with that?"

Dre didn't comment on what Malachi said instead he got out of the car and slammed the door which pissed Malachi off even more. Dre just wanted to get the shit over with, Shay was getting out of the hospital and he needed to be there.

"Damn disrespectful ass muthafucka," he said out loud mainly to himself because he knew that Dre couldn't hear him. Malachi finally got out of the car and hit the button on his key chain so the car's alarm would be accessed. He looked at Dre and wanted to slap the shit out of him but instead he put his hands on Dre's shoulder and led him to the apartment.

When they walked inside of the sparsely furnished living room, Dre looked around and then asked, "Why you had that other lady in a nice place and got my momma in this?"

"Lil nigga, you need to stay in your place. Didn't I tell you about asking all those damn questions? Now shut your damn mouth before I shut it for you."

"Malachi, is that you? Shit, it's about time you brought yourself back home. Damn, where the hell have you been?" Kiara asked while she walked from the back bedroom to the living room. As soon as she stepped foot in the front room and saw Dre, she stopped in her tracks.

"Oh my God. My baby. Malachi you found my baby. Come here and let momma look at you," she cried out and pulled Dre into her arms so she could hug him, but he refused to fall for her bullshit show. She'd never shown him any kind of affection and Dre would be damned if he'd let her use him to entertain Malachi.

Dre's arms remained by his side as Kiara wrapped her arms around his body and squeezed. He thought he was going to be sick on his stomach so he asked, "Can I please use the bathroom?"

Kiara let him go and looked him in the eyes and said, "Yeah son, it's down the hall on the left. When you're through, I'll make you something to eat. You gotta be starving by now." Kiara's words were an understatement because he was more than starving if there was such a thing. He turned and walked slowly down the hall until he found the bathroom and then went in, shut the door and locked it behind him.

***

Justin Valentine had been out of the loop in what seemed like forever. He blamed his absence from the game on his best friend's death. Him and Treyvon Myers had met when they were just seven years old but formed a bond that carried them through their teens and up into adulthood. They started their own organization and ruled it with iron fists. They didn't even allow their workers to be a dollar short. If they were, then they would have to pay the consequences. Justin and Trey had been so close that they even fucked the same hoes sometimes at the same time. Their friendship meant more than any bitch ever could and they never let one come between them.

That had been many years ago and Valentine, as the streets called him, had grown up a lot. He still thought about Trey from time to time. How could he not? He still remembered the night Trey was gunned down and it still broke his heart.

"Damn, my nigga that bitch ain't playin," Valentine said as he watched the trick go down on Trey. His dick was hard from the anticipation of waiting for his turn.

"Hell yeah man, this bitch is suckin shaking the hell outta my shit. Man, why don't you go head and tap that ass instead of waiting on this slow head she giving?"

The two shared a laugh but suddenly stopped when a noise came from outside. Valentine put a finger to his lips telling Trey to be quiet. Trey tapped the woman in front of him on the shoulder and motioned with his hand for her to lift her mouth up off him and she did as he asked. He then reached over and picked up his thirty-eight and got up along with his partner. The woman slid a T-shirt on over her bare breasts and slid down beside the chair that Trey had occupied.

Both men quietly tiptoed to a window but before they could peek out the curtains, the door was kicked in and Tug walked in with a gun pointed directly in front of him. As soon as he noticed Trey, he began to shoot and before Valentine could pop off a shot, Trey was already on the floor with a hole in his chest. Tug felt the bullet as soon as it hit him in the lower back. He had expected Trey to be alone because the trick told him that it would be just him and her. When she got there and realized her and Trey weren't by themselves, it was too late to call anything off.

Tug turned to face Valentine and said through painful gasps, "Nigga I just want what's in the house and I'll leave. I ain't mean to hurt nobody. That bitch told me it was just gonna be her and Trey."

Valentine had forgotten all about the bitch that was just on Trey's dick until Tug gave him that information. He heard the trick as she cried beside the same chair, she had just swallowed his boys manhood in.

When he looked at her, she cried out, "He wasn't supposed to shoot him. I'm sorry. It wasn't supposed to..." The bullet between her eyes silenced her before she could finish her sentence. Valentine turned back to Tug and said, "Nigga you came here to rob my boy but you know that he would have gave it to you. He ain't have to die, bitch."

Tug begged for his life while Valentine pointed the gun at him. "Come on man. I got spooked. I ain't mean to kill him. I ain't even know the gun was loaded. Please man. Please just let me go. I swear you'll never see me again." His shirt was soaked in blood from the hole in his lower back and Valentine could tell he was in pain. However, Val had no compassion for the bastard that took his heart from him. Trey was like his brother and now he had to avenge him.

"You damn right, I'll never see you again," Valentine said right before he put a slug in the middle of the fiend's forehead. When Tug dropped to the floor, Valentine checked to make sure he was dead before going to Trey's side and when he got there, he lifted Trey's head up into his hands. Trey was barely hanging on but managed to say through short breaths, "Yo Val, my nigga. I had a good run, dawg. I love you man. Please, just make sure you look out for Daymion. Don't let the game suck him up like it did me. Man, I know I taught him everything, but I don't' want him to go out like this. Please take care of him, just prom...." Trey began to cough up blood before he could finish his sentence and Valentine held him up a little higher so he wouldn't choke on the liquid.

"Yo Trey, it's all good, man. I got to get you to a hospital. I need you to hold on, though. Aight, dawg. Hold on."

"No. No Val, it's alright man. I'm ready to go. Just do like I asked and take care of my baby brother. Tell that lil nigga I love him. I'll see you when you get there. I, I, I'll see," and then his head fell to the side.

Valentine didn't want to let him go but there was nothing he could do to bring him back. He said out loud, "Don't worry, Trey. I'll take care of him. I love you man." Valentine laid Trey's head back on the carpeted floor and ran his fingers over his eyes to close them but instead of keeping his word to his best friend, he left town and never looked back.

Justin Valentine was now a prominent juvenile law attorney. He wanted to represent those who couldn't fight for themselves. The little black boys who got the short end of the stick and tried to survive on their own only to be a product of the streets. The same streets he had started out in and the same ones that showed him no love back.

Valentine decided that it was time to go back where he'd come from and fulfill the promise he'd made to his best friend all those years ago. He didn't have a wife or kids tying him down. He only had the occasional jump off but nobody special enough to keep him there. Hell, he didn't even know if Daymion Myers was still breathing. He hated leaving the way he did but losing Trey took a lot out of him. If he wouldn't have left, he could have very well ended up like Trey and unlike him, Valentine wasn't ready to die. He hadn't lived his best life yet.

He had already secured a nice two-bedroom condominium on the outskirts of town and was ready to move in. How long he would stay had not been determined. He planned on getting a job with the Justice Department and had already interviewed. He hadn't been told if he got the position yet, but he was pretty sure of himself. He picked up the last of his bags and carried it out to his Yukon Denali and hopped in. He was ready for whatever, but he never could of guessed who would fall into his life and change it forever.

***

"What the hell is taking that little muthafucka so long in the bathroom?" Malachi asked Kiara after some time had passed.

"I 'ont know. Maybe he had to take a shit or something."

"Well get your ass up and go check on him."

Kiara sucked her teeth and pushed her chair away from the table. "Make sure you check on that attitude you for got while you at it."

Kiara walked down the hall to the bathroom door and knocked lightly. "Dre, what's taking you so long? Are you okay in there?" She asked but got no answer. So, she knocked again. This time, a little bit harder. "Dre, what the hell are you doing in there? Bring your ass outta there."

Malachi grew impatient and finally got up out of his chair and went down the hall where Kiara was beating on the bathroom door. He looked at her crazy and asked, "Yo, what's up? Why he ain't opened the door yet?"

"I don't know, Malachi. Maybe he fell and hit his head or something. I don't hear any kind of movement coming from in there."

Malachi pushed Kiara out of the way and grabbed the knob on the door although, he knew it was locked. His nose flared and he told Kiara, "Stand back because I'm about to kick this motherfucker in."

Kiara did as he told her to do and moved away from the door. Malachi then lifted his right leg and kicked the door as hard as he could. The door flew open immediately and Malachi walked in somehow already knowing what he would find. "That little bastard is gone. His ass climbed out the window."

"What? How? That window is not that big."

"Yeah, well it was big enough, bitch."

"Now, why I got to be all that Malachi? Why can't you just talk to me like I'm somebody instead of a piece of shit? I bet you don't talk to that other bitch like that."

The slap came so quick it knocked Kiara off her feet. "Don't you ever talk to me like that again, and there ain't no other bitch, so stop tripping."

"You don't think I know about that bitch you got housed up in a fucking two story house condo Malachi? I know just how y'all niggas from the streets get down. One bitch ain't never enough for y'all, but if you want to keep both of us, at least treat us equally or I can find a motherfucker who will." Kiara got up off the floor and walked away holding her cheek which still stung from Malachi's hand. She went in the bedroom and slammed the door behind her leaving him to think about what she said. Kiara knew that she wasn't going to leave him, but he didn't. All she wanted was a little respect and even if she had to pretend to love Dre to get it, she would.

***

Big Gun swore that he would never cross through a prison gate, but he had no choice. His dawg was behind those gates, and he had to be there for him. Plus, there was things they needed to talk about that couldn't be spoken of through a telephone line. He knew that it could have very well been him living in a two man cell but he had been fortunate enough not to let them crackers run up on him and hem him up.

Big Gun had been in the dope game almost all of his life. It wasn't the plans he'd made when he was a little boy but it was just how things worked out. His momma died giving birth to him and his father was a low level dealer on the corners of the city who had ended up smoking some bad weed. He didn't know the buds had been soaked in battery acid before he smoked it and it caused him to have a seizure. After that, he was never the same so Big Gun had to step up and be the man of the house. He had to feed his father and even bathe and dress him. It was hard for an such a young kid to handle such a big responsibility but Big Gun couldn't imagine anyone else doing it. He loved his father and knew that he was out on them corners to provide for him so he wanted to do the same. His father managed to hold on for a couple of years but the weight of not being able to do anything for himself got the best of him. Big Gun didn't know how he got the strength, but his father got a gun and blew his own brains out one day while Gun was on the block. Big Gun made a vow to never indulge in any kinds of drugs because he didn't want to go out like his father and he had stuck to that vow.

He was so deep in thought that he didn't realize Mellow was standing in front of him. "Yo Gun, my nigga you aight?"

Big Gun snapped out of his thoughts and finally acknowledged his friend's presence. "Ah, my bad. I was just thinking about my pops. How you holding up, Mellow man?"

Big Gun stood and the two shared a brotherly hug and then sat down. Mellow could tell that there was something heavy weighing Gun down, so he asked him straight up, "You seem like you got some shit on your mind it must be real deep for you to come up here. I'm shocked you even had nerve to walk through those gates, G. I preciate it, though."

"Man, I can't let you sit in here and not get no visitation. You my fucking dawg and I told you I was gonna ride. Shit, I know if I was in the same situation, your ass would be sitting in this seat."

"Yeah G, a nigga would ride to hell and back for you. How's shit going out there? Why Teddy fat ass ain't come with you, though?"

Big Gun's expression changed at the sound of Teddy's name. He hated to be the one to bring the bad news especially when Mellow already had a load on him, but he knew it had to be done. "Yo man, Teddy gone."

"The fuck you just say? Nigga, go ahead on with that bullshit and come real with it. Quit playing with me like that."

"My nigga, I wish like hell that I was playing but he gone for real."

Mellow felt the tears but closed his eyes for a minute to stop them and then he asked, "Do you know who did it man? I know you and Dory gonna get the nigga who dropped him, right?"

"I'm sorry Mel, but I'm on my own in this. Dory aint goin do shit because he's the nigga that dropped him."

"What? Nah, man. This shit is too much. The fuck he do that shit for? Teddy was part of the team. How he gonna drop his own man like that?"

"Dory caught Shay stealing out of the pot to help Spade pay his fees. The nigga had Malice jumping his ass and taking his bread, so Teddy and Shay stepped up to help him."

"So, it was Shay ass? Man, that nigga thought it was one of us. Damn."

"Well, when he caught Shay, he beat that ass pretty bad. She told him she was pregnant but he ain't give a fuck. He beat that lil muthafucka out of her. Teddy went to straighten that shit out and instead of killing Dory, he beat his ass and thought he was just gonna walk away. Dory caught him in the head when he was walking out."

"Damn bruh that muthafucka. I know you gonna avenge that shit right?"

Big Gun thought about his question before he answered and then said, "Mellow, you know a nigga want to kill that bastard but I got to play that shit out right. I don't want to fuck around and miss and then end up like Teddy. I'm gonna get him. I'm just waiting for the right time."

They sat and talked for a few minutes and shared a few laughs together. Big Gun asked about the other men that

Mellow was doing time with and that reminded Mellow of the niggas he'd been chilling with.

"Check this. I been chilling with that nigga named Daymion Myers. He a real muthafucka too. Been in for a minute now. You ever heard of him G?"

"Dawg, that Spade's daddy. That nigga got popped on a statutory rape charge fucking with Spade's momma, and when them mufuckas went in his ass was dirty as fuck."

"Damn man. That's some sucka ass shit that bitch did to him. He coming out in a couple months next year. I think you should fuck with the nigga."

"Yeah man, I might be able to do that. Go ahead and hook the nigga with my digits and I'll see what I can do for him. Does he know Spade runs with the crew?"

"That's what's funny. I mentioned Dre but he ain't say shit about being his daddy. You sure about that information?"

"Yeah, nigga I'm sure. Maybe you need to see what's up with that? You saying that muthafucka real but he obviously keeping something back and you need to find out what it is before you send him my way."

"I'm on it, G. I'm gonna get some answers and I'll let you in on it."

"Yeah well, you do that. We need to know if he's gonna walk with us because if not, I'm a need to have my gat ready to lay his ass down."

When visitation was over, the two shared one more friendly hug and parted ways. Mellow wasn't sure what Daymion was holding but he was about to find out.

***

Kayla was not impressed with Dory's bad boy swagger because honestly, she found his ass weak. All she cared about was him telling her where Dre was and she'd be on her way.

It had been a minute since she'd been with a man and she couldn't lie to herself, her womanhood throbbed with anticipation but she already knew that only Daymion Myers could satisfy it. Dory put it on thick and tried really hard to cuff her but Kayla was far from desperate.

She took a long hot shower and tried to enjoy it but she was too worried about Dre. She hoped Dory was telling her the truth about not knowing where he was at. She finally got out the shower and lotioned her pale skin down with apricot essence. She skipped the perfume because it would have just been over kill. She wrapped one of the large beach towels around her nakedness right before she heard the phone. She already knew who would be on the other end so she answered immediately.

"Hello."

"You have a collect call from an inmate in the Department of Corrections. To accept this call press one now".

Kayla pressed the number one with a smile on her face.

"Aye yo Kayla where you been at baby? A nigga needs to see that pretty face again."

Kayla walked out of her bedroom with the towel still around her and the phone pressed to her ear. She sat on the couch and leaned back so she could talk to her man.

"Hey baby, a bitch sure does miss you but I'll be back up there this weekend. I can't wait to come up there and pick you up instead."

"Well you wont be waiting much longer but what you doing right now?"

"I actually just got out of the shower and because of you I haven't even had the chance to get dressed."

Daymion heard what she said and imagined her paleness against his darkness. He could almost feel her perky pink nipples between his lips while he teased them with his tongue. His dick rocked up just from the sound of her voice so he knew his nut sack would be ready to bust when she was actually beside him. He admired her womanly curves every time she came to visit and he couldn't wait to taste her creamy vanilla juices.

"So that just means a nigga caught you right on time."

"Hhhmmm, maybe. Depends on what you're going to do about it."

"Well, a man like me might just have a plan for that but I ont know if you ready for all this. I aint like them otha niggas you done dealt with."

She smiled and unwrapped the towel from around her. She spread her legs and her lover lips opened instantly. She then placed a finger over her swollen pearl and imagined it being his tongue.

"MMM, Daymion baby, this pussy is waiting for you but a bitch like me needs you to talk me through this orgasm, I'm about to get just from hearing your voice. You think you can make this pussy cum?"

"You aint said nothing but a word because a thug like me knows just what to say to wet it up."

She could have sworn that she came about four times but couldn't be sure because she was so far gone she had lost track.

"A nigga gonna put a baby up in there when I get home."

She giggled and stood to her feet and walked back to her bedroom. "Of course I'm ready. I can't wait to share everything with you."

Before he could get another word out the operator came back on the line, "You have one minute remaining on this call! Thank you for using securelink."

The two said their goodbyes and hung up. Kayla dropped her phone on the bed and jumped up and down like a schoolgirl with her first crush. Daymion had opened up something she had closed off long ago. She wished the moment could last forever because she didn't remember ever being so happy. She hoped that he was serious about them having a child together. She was ready to be a mother and she couldn't think of anyone else she'd rather share the experience with.

Chapter 13

Dre was glad that he had been able to fit through the small bathroom window. There was no way he was going to be locked up in that apartment with Malachi and his mother. He did want to ask her why she had moved without even looking for him to let him know but he didn't want to talk around her new man. He knew that the window would be his only escape, but he also knew that he had to get out of the streets before Malachi came looking for him.

He was almost to the block he served on and when he turned the corner, he heard someone call him. "Aye yo. What's up? Where the hell you been at?" Kendrick asked when he appeared. Dre stood still for a minute to wait for Malice to show up but when he didn't, he relaxed a little and responded, "Where's your partner at?"

Kendrick sucked his teeth and stated, "Man, I 'ont hang with that muthafucka no more. I ain't down with that shit he was doing to you. That shit wasn't cool. You just out here trying to make it too."

"How you know what I'm out here trying to do you ont know me nigga."

Kendrick laughed and held his hands out in front of him and said, "Whoa playa. I ain't mean anything by it so chill. Aight."

"Well, I don't got no money so you ain't getting nothing out of me today."

"Man, I ain't here for no money. I been looking for you to call a truce. I say we form a little brotherhood and get down together."

"Well, what do you think your friend is gonna say to that? He ain't gonna like me hanging around all the time besides I aint fuckin with his ass."

"I ain't fucking with him like that no more. I already told you that. It's just gonna be you and me. Oh, and my little sister, Tasha. What you think?"

"Your sister. Man, you sure you wanna bring a female in on this? They say them bitches be the ones telling everythang. I ain't trying to get caught up."

"Nigga, my sister ain't no bitch. Besides, she gonna ride with me all the way. She could make our pickups because a girl is less likely to get stopped by the man."

"Our pickups? you got someone that fucks with you .and your sister like that?"

"Hell yeah and I plan on putting his black ass outta business one day."

"Then, where we gonna get our shit from?"

"We gonna get it from my boy Cardo across town, and we gonna get paid. You ain't making shit fucking with Dory greedy ass so you might as well come on board with me. What do you say?"

Before Dre could answer him, a car pulled up beside them. Neither of them knew if they should run or not but before they had a chance to decide, the tinted window rolled down.

Dre smiled when he saw who it was, "Shay"

"Hey Dre. I'm sorry I haven't been around but you know the deal. Why didn't you come see me?"

"Shay, I couldn't bare to come up there and see you like that. That shit would have broke something in me. You okay, though?"

"Yeah, I'm good. Just missing Teddy."

"I miss him too. I wish I could have done something to help him but I aint have no weapon on me. I'm sorry Shay."

"It's okay. It's all part of the game. You just never know it's your time until it happens."

"Are you gonna take Dory back again knowing what he did to Teddy?"

Shay had no intentions of ever getting back with Dory but she had to see him one more time so she could give him a few choice words and to let him know that he didn't break her soul, only her heart.

"I'm actually headed to see Dory right now. I mean, not to make up or anything. I would never be with that bastard again, but I need some closure. You wanna ride with me? I could sure use the company."

Dre thought about her question and then answered, "Yeah, I'll go. I need to let him know that I'm pulling up out of the crew. I'm on some better shit now." He turned turned to Kendrick and said, "Hey, I'll meet you back here in a couple of hours and we can go handle what you was talking about."

"Bet that. I'll see you later, kid," Kendrick replied.

Dre looked at him crazy and whispered, "Yo man, don't call me kid in front of my future wife. Know what I'm saying?"

Kendrick laughed and said, "Yeah Dre, I got you."

Dre walked around to the passenger side of Shay's car and got in. He was ready to be free of Dory just like Shay was. True enough, Dory did help him out but he had underlying evil in his heart. Dre had never figured out why Dory started treating him dirty but he no longer cared because he would no longer be in his reach.

He wondered how Dory was going to act when he heard the news of him pulling out. He remembered Dory telling him that once you were in the crew there was no leaving but Dre would be damned if he was forced to stay. He was ready for the move he was about to make. He only hoped that Shay was ready too.

***

"Aye man, what's up? Can a nigga holla at you for a minute?" Mellow asked Daymion as soon as he saw him on the court.

"Sure." He then turned to the other men on the court and excused himself. "Hey, y'all gonna have to put someone in my place for a minute. A nigga needs an intermission."

"Yeah, dawg, you good."

"Yo, Follow, come play in his spot."

Daymion walked off the court and grabbed a towel so he could wipe the sweat off of his face and arms. He then grabbed a Styrofoam cup from the sleeve on the bench and filled it with water so he could wet his throat. He walked to Mellow and the two gave each other dap and walked to another bench a little farther from the rest of the inmates playing ball. Once they were seated and out of ear shot, Day asked, "Damn nigga, what's up? You aight? You seem like you got some deep shit on your mind. Was it all good at your visit, man?"

Mellow let out a sigh and didn't beat around the bush with his question. "Yo, Day, my nigga when you was gonna tell me that Dre was your son?"

Daymion was thrown off with his question. He never wanted Mellow to find out because he feared that something would happen to his boy. However, since word was out, he figured he'd answer Mellow's question truthfully. "Dawg, I ain't gonna lie or sugarcoat shit but I was afraid that if you knew, it would put my son in danger." Daymion then became emotional. "Man, I only met the lil nigga twice in his life. The first time was when he came out his momma's pussy and

143

then I ain't seen him again until recently and he just turned seventeen years old. That's a lot of time without him in my life and I just couldn't imagine putting him in harm's way and something happening to him. Hell, his fuck ass momma apparently does enough of that."

Mellow could feel the sincerity in Daymion's voice, "Yo Day, the crew got love for Spade. We would never put him in a situation like that. At least not on purpose, and I ain't trying to make you feel worse, but I honestly can't say the same about Dory. If it will make you feel better, I'm a call my boy Big Gun and tell him to pull ya boy outta there. Dory ass can be foul and now that Teddy gone, I worry about the kid too."

"Teddy? Who the hell was Teddy?"

"Man, Teddy wasn't nothing but a big ole soft ass muthafucka but that was our boy. Gun told me at visitation that Dory put a hot one in the back of his dome for kicking his ass. Ya kid was there when it happened but ain't no harm come to him. Lil nigga ain't been seen since, though. Gun gonna locate him and make sure he stays away."

"Nigga, if something happens to my son, I'm a kill that bastard as soon as I step outta these gates. That bitch is using my boy to get to me as a form of payback for killing his bitch. Pussy ass fuckboy got to see me, though."

They continued to talk for a while with Daymion explaining to Mellow where the beef with him and Dory stemmed from. Mellow was a real nigga and understood why Dory held back on the information about Dre. He felt bad for Daymion and made a vow to do everything within his power to ensure that Dory didn't get his hands back on him, because just because Mellow was locked in, he would never completely be locked out.

***

Shay pulled into Dory's driveway slowly because in all honesty, she was a little afraid. She was still healing from the beating he had put on her and still grieved from the loss of the baby he had made her lose. Although, the baby would have had a piece of shit for a father, Shay would have still loved it the same and had already gotten used to it being a part of her. Dre could see her hesitation when the car came to a stop and the engine was turned off.

"What's wrong, Shay? We going in or not? You aint got to be scared of that nigga no more I got you." Dre pulled a gun from the back of his pants and held it up.

Shay looked at him. "Where in the hell did you get that from Dre? You don't need to be walking around with that on you. Nothing at all is going to happen in there so you wont be needing it. I'm just preparing my heart. Dory's ass has broken it into little, tiny pieces since we been together. I'm just hoping that I'll be able to put it back together and move on. I hope that one day I can actually love again."

"Don't worry, I'll be here to help you repair all the damage. I'm a teach you how to love again. You can always depend on me because I'll never hurt you."

"Oh Dre, honey, you have such a kind heart. I'm glad that I can depend on you, and I hope that you are always a part of me."

A silence filled the small space between them until Dre spoke again, "Well, I hope you know that one day I'm gonna marry you."

"Oh yeah, well when was you gonna inform me that I had a fiancé?"

Dre smiled at her and said, "I just did."

Shay laughed but deep in her heart, she knew he was serious. He was still young though, and she knew that at any moment he could meet someone who would steal his heart away. She would give him a few more years and see where his heart was then.

"Alright Dre, let's go in here and give Dory's ass a piece of our mind. You ready for this?"

"Yeah Shay, I'm ready, and don't worry, I got your back."

Deep down, Shay knew that he did.

The two of them got out quietly just in case Dory was asleep, and if he was, Shay decided they would find something really hard and beat his ass together. She didn't want Dre going in the house shooting even though she knew he preferred it that way. When Shay stuck her key in the door, she was surprised to find that he hadn't changed the locks which to her meant that he anticipated her return.

Dre walked in closely behind her. It was dark in the living room, but Shay knew her way around from so many nights of being there and tonight would be no different. They walked further into the room and when they did there was no mistaking what they heard.

"Yes, Dory baby. Mmm, you feel so good inside of me. Please don't stop."

Dre shook his head because he ain't believe that Dory already had a bitch in Shay's place. Shay looked at him funny and then finished leading the way to the bedroom where they would find Dory and his company.

Shay opened the door slowly and saw Dory's black ass. His muscles flinched every time he pushed into the woman in front of him. She remembered how good his dick game was and knew that the woman was in deep sexual bliss. Shay's womanhood throbbed from the sound of Dory's sex moans. The sweat that rolled down him made her wet even though she tried to fight it. Dory has been her first, so she had no one to compare him to and she was fine with that.

She had forgotten all about Dre until he stepped from behind her and studied the couple. He walked up closer to the bed and when Shay grabbed his hand to pull him back, he yanked it out of her grasp. The couple still in their own world never ever felt him come up on them until it was too late. Dre had the tip of the gun on Dory's temple before he could even think to blink.

"Pull outta that bitch and face your mufucking destiny nigga."

Dory thought he was hearing things but turned to the familiar voice anyway. He couldn't believe that Dre had a gun pointed at him and slowly pulled out of the woman.

"The fuck is you doin in my house? And what the hell do you want? Don't you see me doing grown man shit here."

The woman covered her naked body and slid up close to the headboard. She was scared and ashamed all at the same time. She just couldn't believe that she had gotten caught up like that.

"Yeah nigga but that grown man shit bout to land you in an early grave?"

Dory and the woman didn't even realize that Shay was in the room too. They had been so focused on Dre that they didn't pay attention to anything else. But sudden movement caused the woman to turn her head and when she did she noticed the pretty black girl with the mocha skin.

"Dory, who is that at the door?"

Dory turned his head and finally saw Shay.

"Bitch, you got some nerve to show your thieving ass back up here. Have you done lost your damn mind?"

"Dory, you know her? Who is she to you?"

"Bitch, you want to know who the hell I am? I'll tell you. I was just in that same spot that your ass is in. That was until he beat my ass and put me in a hospital. I was his bitch a week ago, but you don't gotta worry about me no more. You can have his sorry dirty dick ass. As a matter of fact, don't stop what y'all was doing on our account. Go head Dory, let a bitch watch you in action."

"Shit, you should bring your ass on in the bed with us. This bitch here might be able to teach you a thing or two. My dick ain't never been sucked so good," Dory stated and started stroking his manhood. He then laughed and added, "Remember how good this dick was to you, Shay? Remember how a nigga use to be in them guts? Yeah, you won't never forget, will you? Bitch, I was good to you. You ain't have to take from me, and all for this lil muthafucka right here."

Dre cocked the gun and his nostrils flared in anger at the disrespect he had spit at Shay. The woman tried to get out the bed, but Dory pushed her back down and said, "Your ass ain't going nowhere. These muthafuckas wanna stay and watch, then let them but I'm about to finish what I started so come on and boot that fat ass up. This lil nigga aint gon do shit with that piece in his hand."

"Um Dory, please just let me get up and get dressed."

"Fuck that. You can get dressed after I nut all in that pussy. Now, come on."

She slid down in the bed and spread her legs so Dory could finish what he'd started. She felt her heartbeat quicken, "Please Dory let me go, I don't know what's going on here and I don't want to know I just want to leave."

"Ya know what? Take your ass on then. Pussy aint all that anyway. Scary ass bitch. I need a mufuckin rider and you just proved that you aint one. Get the fuck outta here."

The woman jumped out the bed and grabbed her clothes but didn't put them on. Instead she wrapped herself in the sheet and ran out leaving her shoes behind. Dory got up and pulled on some boers and sat on the end of the bed. He didn't think Dre would really shoot him so he wasn't worried.

He figured Dre to be a coward like his father. He had known from the beginning that Dre had a thing for Shay but he would have to get his paper up to keep a bitch like her but what he didn't know was that it wasn't his money she was after.

***

"Aye yo, Tasha, we bout to make that paper. I hope you ready to get paid," Kendrick said out loud when he walked in his little sister's room. He noticed that Tasha was lying on the bed crying and wondered what was wrong with her. "Tasha, yo what's going on with you. You aight?"

He went to her side because he was deeply concerned. He loved his little sister and had only seen her cry one time before and that was when their grandpa died two years earlier. Tasha was usually a free spirit and always had a smile on her face so for her to be crying something serious had to have happened.

"Kendrick, I , I, I lost my baby."

"What? What damn baby? Girl, you trippin. What the hell are you talking about?"

Tasha sat up in the bed and looked at her big brother. She wondered if he would still love her the same after she told him what had happened. "I got pregnant, and I just miscarried the baby. I went to use the bathroom and when I got up, the toilet was full of blood."

"Pregnant? When the hell did you start having sex? I thought you were a virgin still. Who the hell got you pregnant, Tasha? I'm a kill they ass." Kendrick asked angrily. His little innocent baby sister had gotten herself knocked up and it pissed him off.

"I, I was a virgin Kenny, but I was out back hanging out the laundry and your friend Malice came up and pushed me down. He tried to get with me but when I refused him, he pulled my clothes down and took it. I ended up pregnant but now it's gone." Tasha began to cry again.

"What? Malice raped you and you just now telling me this shit. Why the hell ain't you been said something, Tasha? I'm a kill his black ass." Kendrick jumped off the bed from beside her and paced the floor.

"I'm sorry, Kenny. I wanted to tell you, but I didn't want you to be mad at me and I didn't want to start any drama with you and your friend."

"My friend. That fuck nigga ain't my friend. How the hell he gonna put his hands on you? His bitch ass knows how I feel about you. I'm a kill his ass."

"No Kenny. Please just let it go. Please. I don't want you to go to jail because of me." Tasha cried while she pled with her brother not to do the unthinkable. She knew that eventually he would have found out she was carrying a baby because regardless of how it was created, she was going to keep it. Kendrick and Malice had been friends for a while, and she hated to come between their friendship, but she couldn't lie to the one person who had her back.

"Don't worry, sis. I ain't gonna go to jail. I would never leave you out here to fend for yourself but that muthafucka must pay for what he done to you. I can't let that shit slide."

She understood the position she had put Kendrick in, and she also understood that there was no talking him out of it. "Please, Kenny. Please just promise me that you'll be careful. You know Malice's brother is crazy and he gonna come looking for you if he finds out you done something to him."

"That nigga can get it too if he gets in my fuckin way," Kenny said and pulled the gun from the waist of his jeans.

"Oh my God, Kenny. Where did you get that from?"

"Don't ask no questions, sis. The less you know, the better off you'll be. You just stay in the house and lock all the doors and windows until I come back for you. Don't let nobody up in this bitch," Kendrick said and then walked out of her bedroom shutting the door behind him. Kendrick was on a murder mission. However, he didn't know he would have a soldier on his side. One that would save him from being the victim instead.

Chapter 14

"Bitch, take your ass out there and find your son. What type of mother lets her child be in the streets like that? If that pussy wasn't on point, I'd put your ass back on the pole," Malachi said and then walked in the bedroom. He slammed the door and locked it behind him. He was tired of Kiara's sorry ass. She seemed to only be good for sucking his dick and giving him something wet to dip in. He couldn't even believe why a nigga like Daymion Myers had ever fucked with a bitch like her. If given the same option, Malachi was sure that he would have chosen prison too.

Kiara banged on the door and cried out, "Come on Malachi, open the door. I told you his black ass was bad and needed some discipline. Shit it's hard raising a son by myself. His fuck ass daddy should've done right by me and then maybe he would've been around to raise him."

The door was suddenly yanked open and Malachi grabbed Kiara by the throat. His hand seemed to fit around it perfectly and he could see himself taking the life out of the bitch. However, he was on a mission and Kiara was part of his plan. Daymion would be out soon and the first person he would seek out would be her, so he had to keep her and her bastard around until the ultimate prize dropped in his hands.

Malachi pushed Kiara against the wall and removed his hand. He pulled her lips into his and kissed her hard.

"Mmm," she moaned with pleasure and reached her hand in his jeans so she could feel the greatest pleasure she'd been given. She didn't know how any woman could ever survive without some good dick. Kiara pulled his manhood through the zipper and stroked it slowly. "Turn around," he said, and Kiara listened. As soon as her back was to him, he pulled her shorts down and entered her pussy roughly.

"Uh, Malachi." She cried out in pleasure. He was already worked up, so it didn't take him long to reach his peak.

When he released himself inside of her, he pulled out and walked back into the room closing the door behind him.

"Really, Malachi? You know what? Fuck you. I'm outta here." Kiara pulled her shorts back up and without even cleaning off the juices Malachi left behind, she walked out. She was on a mission to find Dre and when she did, she was going to beat his ass for putting her in a fucked-up position once again. She needed Dre to hang on to Malachi because for some reason, he had a deep interest in him. Kiara didn't care what it was, she only cared about securing her position under the nigga she had given up everything for.

Malachi breathed a sigh of relief when he heard the front door slam. He just wanted to sit back and relax without any drama. Suddenly, thoughts of Malia came to his mind. "Damn baby, I miss you but a nigga gonna see you soon. I got to pay that muthafucka back first, though. I gave you my word and I'm gonna keep it."

When Malia first told him that she was pregnant, it bought joy to his heart. She had been the first woman he had ever felt real true love for. However, she had some baggage by the name of Dorian Thompson, and she found it hard to get rid of him. Malachi offered to eliminate him from earth, but Malia begged him to back off. Dorian thought the baby she carried was his, but she was going to confess and tell him that it belonged to someone else.

Malachi and Malia were young and in love and all they wanted was to spend their lives together.

"I'm gonna end things with him tonight, Mally. I can't continue to see him knowing how much I'm hurting you. I love you," Malia said while Malachi held her in his arms.

He kissed her on the forehead and said, "Don't move from this spot. I got something for you."

Malia giggled at the thought because he was always surprising her with little gifts to show his love but what he didn't know was that he never had to give her anything to show it because she could feel it even when they were apart. Malia anxiously awaited his return and when he walked back in the room, he kissed her on the forehead once more and then dropped to one knee.

He pulled out a small red box and Malia could feel her heart speed up. "Oh my God," she said and covered her mouth with her hands. Malachi held the box in front of her and opened it to reveal a heart shaped five carat diamond ring.

"Malia, I know we are still young, but I want to grow old with you. Together, we have created a life and I can't wait to meet him or her we were blessed to be given another chance at being parents. I love you and I promise that you will never have to question that. I'm a be loyal to you for life. Alright, that's enough romance, you gonna marry a nigga or what?"

Malia laughed and then wrapped her arms around his neck and cried.

"Whoa, whoa what's with the tears?"

She replied, "I just love you so much Malachi and these are happy tears."

"Well, you still haven't answered my question. Will you marry me?"

"Yes, Malachi. Yes."

Malachi didn't even realize he was crying. He loved Malia with everything he had inside of him. He just couldn't believe that she was really gone. He had tried over the years to replace her, but no other woman compared. Her murder had taken so much out of him including his heart. He was still trying to heal from his grief but he knew that he wouldn't be able to until he avenged her death. It wouldn't be long before Daymion Myers would be a free man and Malachi vowed to be there when he walked out of them gates. He was going to send him straight to hell where he belonged.

***

Dre walked out of the room and left Shay with Dory even though, he wasn't happy about it. He didn't want to disappoint Shay so he did all she asked of him but he would be on standby. As he was running through the living room, a shiny object caught his eye. He stopped and turned around and thought about his next move. He looked back toward the door that he had just ran out of and then back to the object. The decision he made would change everything, but hell what did he have to lose? Dre could hear Shay going off on Dory and he feared for her safety. He knew that Dory was a loose cannon and could go off at any moment. The things he imagined Dory doing to Shay were unthinkable and he knew that he had to protect her. His head was spinning in so many different directions, but he had to make a choice before it was too late. Dre picked up the gun and held it tightly. His gun wasn't loaded but he knew for a fact that the one he had just found was full. It seemed so big in his hands. He had never held one before, but he knew of the power that existed inside of it.

It was the same gun that Dory had shot Teddy down with. Dre could still see visions of his mentor and it saddened him. If only he would have been braver, he could have helped Teddy, but he was too weak. It seemed as if the screaming got louder and then Dre heard a loud thud. His heart sped up and he thought he would go into cardiac arrest. "I'm coming,

Shay," he said out loud. Although, he knew she couldn't hear him. He promised her that he would always have her back and he meant it.

When Dre opened the bedroom door back up, he looked for Shay and found her on the floor where he assumed Dory had put her he continuously punched her and when he ripped her shirt off Dre had seen enough.

"Let her up, Dory."

Dory had thought he left and was surprised to hear his voice. Dory asked without even turning around to face him. "And if I don't what the hell you gonna do about it?"

"Turn around and find out bitch."

Dory laughed but turned around. When he saw the gun pointed at him, he laughed harder. "Lil nigga, you ain't gonna do shit with it. Your fuckin balls ain't big enough." Then, he really went in. "Didn't your daddy ever teach you that if you point a gun at a muthafucka you better use it? Oh, my bad. I forgot. Your daddy locked the fuck up and can't teach your dumb ass shit. So what you gonna do, you fucking coward? You aint do shit to help Teddy so do you think I'm worried about you now. Huh?"

Dory started to walk closer to Dre, but Dre held his stance. Shay Kayla cried out, "Dre, Dre please put the gun down. You don't understand what you're doing. Please."

Dre said with a hatred filled voice, "I use to look up to you, thought you was gonna help be something out there but how can you help me when you aint shit yourself."

"Nigga I aint ask your ass to step to me. That was your choice. Finding out Myers was your father was the icing on the cake. That mufucka killed my seed so before he even had a chance to breathe and to me all is fair in love and war."

***

It had been a minute since Kiara took a hit off the pipe. She never considered herself a crack head but she did enjoy the feeling. She smoked a little weed with Malachi from time to time, but she needed something a little stronger now. Malachi had turned out to be just as bad as all the other niggas she had fucked. She just couldn't understand why she couldn't find a man that wanted to settle down and wife her.

"Muthafuckas only wanna use a bitch to get they dick off. I'm tired of that shit," Kiara said to herself on the way to the block. She turned the corner a little too fast and when she did, her competition stared back at her.

Bree couldn't believe her luck. Malachi's other bitch was staring her in the face. She had waited to run into her one day because she wanted to see what he had been laying up with. All she had ever saw was Kiara's face so now, she had a chance to check her all the way out and Kiara definitely didn't disappoint. She was pretty and thick in all the right places.

Kiara had heard Bree's name before but she had never seen her, so she wondered why the female was looking at her funny. "What the hell you looking at me like that for? Bitch, I like dick."

"Oh please. Don't flatter yourself, Kiara."

"How the hell do you know my name? Bitch, you don't know me."

"Hmm yeah. Well, you should be familiar with me by now since you taste me every time you suck Malachi's dick."

"Bree."

"Yeah, so at least I'm not a stranger anymore. How do I taste?"

"Fuck you. Bitch, that nigga comes home to me every night so I ain't studying your ass."

"He may come home to you at night but bitch, he doesn't go until he fucks me. How does it feel to be a second choice?"

Kiara bowed up and pushed Bree and right before Bree swung, a smooth chocolate brown arm came between them.

"Ladies, ladies, now come on there's enough of me to go around. Ain't no need to fight."

Trap Town had just got back from a trip to Miami where he attended his grandfather's funeral. A lot had happened since he'd been gone but he knew that life had to move on. He had noticed the two women about to fight on his way to Dory's. He was about to keep it moving but decided that he could possibly charm himself into a piece of pussy, perhaps two if he got real lucky.

He recognized Kiara Taylor from Kronics from bouncing on his boy's dick, but he wasn't familiar with the other one who looked to be mixed with something foreign.

"Nigga don't flatter yourself, you ain't all that," Bree said with an attitude.

"Yeah, well you ain't stopped checking me out since I been standing in front of you so I must be something."

"You alright, but I agree with her, you ain't all that," Kiara said with a flirtatious smile.

"Oh, so now at least y'all agreeing on something. That's a start. What y'all out here about to fight for anyway? And don't tell me it's about a nigga because there are plenty to go around."

When neither of them answered, he knew that he was right. "Yo, for real. Why y'all wanna be greedy? If you are fighting over a nigga, then that means y'all both done been with the nigga. So, you might as well keep sharing him. Shit, y'all come ride with me and I'll make y'all forget all about that chump."

His comment caused both of them to chuckle and Trap hoped that they would take him up on his offer. He had anything they could have wanted cash, drugs, and good dick.

"So, what's up? Y'all ain't got nothing to say? How about it?"

The two women looked at each other and Bree finally spoke up, "You know Kiara, he is right. We been fuckin the same nigga so we might as well accept it. He a dog ass motherfucker anyway so why don't we go enjoy ourselves and forget about his ass for a minute."

Kiara smiled at the thought of having one up on Malachi and agreed, "Alright, I'm down. Let's go have some fun. Shit, what we gotta lose?"

The three of them jumped into Trap Town's car and went to get a room so they could get their minds off the drama in their lives. However, little did they know that the motel they chose was one they should have avoided.

***

"Oh my God, oh my God," Shay cried out when Dory's body hit the floor. She looked at Dre who just stood there with a smirk on his face. "Come on, help me. Maybe we can save him. I think he's still breathing."

Instead of helping Dory, Dre decided to help out another way. He went to the picture that hung above the shoe rack and removed it revealing a safe underneath.

"What, what are you doing? If we don't help him, he's gonna die."

"So, let that bastard die. He don't give a fuck about either of us. If it was you on that floor, his ass would walk out and never look back."

"I know you're mad because of how he's treated me but don't hold that against him. You'll regret it for the rest of your life if he dies when you could have saved him."

Dre stopped what he was doing and turned to Shay "Let me tell you something. I'm happy to be rid of his ass. You can be sad have him but I can assure you that you're not the only one who will. Let that motherfucker die. You'll regret it if you don't."

Dre went back to the wall safe and opened it and then found a brown paper bag and filled it up. He left only the scales behind. He would package the dope up later and give some to Kendrick to help get rid of.

Dre was so engrossed in what was in the safe that he almost didn't hear the sirens until they were right in front of the house. He sped up his pace and then turned to Shay who was still holding out hope for Dory. Shay bent down beside him and looked at Dre. Dory was barely conscious but knew that he would understand her next words, "Bleed out bitch. Karma's a muthafucka."

***

Dre ran as fast as he could after the cops pulled up. -Shay had went ahead of him in her car and he hoped that she was okay.

Dre had never felt so alone in his life and yet he had been alone every day. He wondered if he should get rid of the gun that he had just shot Dory with but something inside of him told him to keep it. At least for a minute.

"Huh muthafucka? You thought you was gonna rape my sister and get away with it. Bitch nigga she was a virgin."

Dre could hear Kendrick's voice through the bushes and moved a little closer. He took his hand and pushed the green leaves to the side so he could see what was going on. He saw Malice on the ground with Kendrick on his stomach punching him. Malice finally got a hit in and knocked Kendrick off of him. Malice then began kicking Kendrick in the stomach and he tried to curl up in a fetal position to stop the blows but he just could not escape them.

"Muthafucka, that bitch asked for it. She liked having this big black dick inside of her. Shit, her hoe ass was begging for it."

Malice was getting the best of Kendrick and Dre knew that he had to do something. He pulled the gun he had used on Dory out of the waist of his jeans. He didn't even know if there were bullets left in it but hoped that it wouldn't come to that. He just wanted to scare Malice and pay him back for the times he had jumped on him. Slowly, Dre emerged from the bushes and walked up on the two of them.

"Leave him alone."

Malice was about to kick Kendrick again but stopped when he heard a voice from behind him. He slowly turned around to see who had the nerve to tell him what to do. When he saw that it was Dre, he laughed at him and said, "Fuck you. Who's gonna make me?"

Dre replied, "I am," and then pulled out the gun that he was holding in his hand from behind his back. He pointed it at Malice, but it wasn't enough to stop the bully.

Malice laughed even harder and then taunted him, "Come on pussy, shoot me."

Dre didn't want to be a murderer, but he was tired of getting shitted on. He knew that if there was a bullet still in the gun, he could end Malice's life with it. He hated him just that much. Malice began to walk closer to Dre and had forgotten all about Kendrick, but as soon as Malice reached for Dre's gun, Kendrick reminded him of his presence.

"Don't even think about it," Kendrick said and pointed the gun he had in his hand. He was so focused on beating his ex-friends ass for the violation on his sister that. He had forgotten that he'd even had it on him until Dre showed up and brandished one. He held the gun steady to the back of his ex-friend's head as if he'd done something like that before.

"Your bitch ass ain't gonna shoot me either. Don't neither one of you got the guts to pull the trigger," Malice said with a laugh.

"I don't wanna kill you, Mal but I will if you make me. I did want to hurt you when I first came here for what you did to my sister, though, but killing you would only hurt her worse because then she'd lose me."

"Man, fuck you and your sister."

Kendrick hit Malice with the butt of the gun and knocked him to the ground. Blood ran down the side of his face from the wound and yet, he still talked shit.

"Man, you hit like a bitch and if you don't kill me, you and your bitch ass sister gonna pay for this. You better do what you need to do now. Nigga, I ain't scared to die."

"My sister got pregnant from what you did to her. She was never gonna tell me what happened, but I walked in on her after she had a miscarriage in the toilet. She was gonna keep that bastard you put inside of her, but she was spared from having the devil's offspring."

Kendrick could feel himself getting emotional but didn't want Malice to see it. However, him and Malice had been friends for a long time and he knew him like a book.

"Go on soft ass nigga and cry. Let them tears fall like a little bitch. You think I give a fuck about your sister getting pregnant and losing it? Huh? She don't mean shit to me and if she would have carried it and had it, she still wouldn't have meant shit."

"Kill him, Kendrick. If you don't kill him, he just gonna come back and get all of us. We can't let him walk away from here tonight," Dre said because he knew what the consequences would be if him and Kendrick let Malice go. It would be even worse for him if Malice found out that he'd shot his brother a little earlier.

Kendrick looked from Dre to Malice and then put a bullet in the chamber of the gun he held out in front of him.

"Go head man. Do it. Do it and let's get the hell outta here."

Kendrick put his finger on the trigger and then closed his eyes. He quickly opened them back up and looked Malice in the eyes. Memories of the way they used to be before came back to him and he put the gun down and said, "I can't. I can't kill him."

As soon as he lowered the gun, another voice appeared.

"You can't but I can," and then Tasha pulled the trigger.

Chapter 15

Dory woke up feeling like he'd been hit by a semi-truck. He looked around and wondered where he was and why he was there. He heard the machines beeping and turned his head toward them, but he was confused at what he saw. "The fuck," he said out loud and tried to get up, but his legs wouldn't move.

The woman opened her eyes from the noise and when she saw Dory trying to get out of the bed, she jumped up out of the chair she had fallen asleep in.

"Dory, oh God. You're awake. I'm so glad you finally woke up."

Dory was confused because he didn't remember the bitch or being brought there. He looked at her funny and asked, "Who the hell are you? Why am I in the hospital?"

She was disappointed but the doctor told her that Dory could possibly have a temporary setback on a lot of things including what he remembered. "You don't remember me? I'm KaPrice."

"If I remembered you, I wouldn't be asking who the hell you were. Now tell me why the fuck I'm attached to all these fucking machines."

Dory might not have remembered much but one thing was for sure, he still had the fucked-up attitude that he had before.

Before KaPrice could answer, the room door opened, and Big Gun walked in.

"Yo, Yo, Yo. What's up my nigga? I ain't think your ass was gonna ever wake up. 'Bout damn time. How you feel man?"

It took Dory a minute, but he remembered Big Gun.

"Gun, man what the hell is going on? What the fuck am I doing here? Tell me something, G."

"Ah, dawg, someone busted in your shit and robbed you and as always, your ass thought you was bulletproof." Big Gun lied about what happened mainly to protect Dre and Shay. Enough blood had been shed and he was trying to keep it from being anymore.

"So, do we know who did it?" Dory asked.

Big Gun and KaPrice looked at each other and then Gun answered him, "Nah, dawg. They just ran in while you were by yourself. Nobody is talking either. You know how the streets do. Niggas be scared to talk and shit, but don't none of that matter now. You alive and that's what counts."

"Yo man, who the hell is this?" Dory asked in a low whisper trying to not be heard but KaPrice was standing too close not to catch the verbal exchange.

"How the hell you don't remember something so pretty? That's some bitch you been fucking your girl, dawg. She should be all you remember?"

"Yeah, you'd think so, but I don't mind getting to know you better. What you say?" Dory asked KaPrice who smiled and said, "I'd like that, Dory. It would be kinda like a fresh start for both of us."

Dory then turned to Gun and asked, "Man, go ask them muthafuckas when they gonna let my ass outta here? Shit, the only way I'm a stay laid up in a bed is if I got a warm body lying beside me."

All three shared a laugh because Dory sounded like his old self. "Man, move out the way so I can at least get up and move my legs a little."

"Uh Dory, I'm not sure that's a good idea. At least right now."

"Man, you tripping, move out the way." Dory tried to move his legs so he could get up and walk around but no matter how hard he tried, they would just not cooperate. "Man, what the fuck going on. These bitches got jokes. My legs tied down or something. What's up Gun? What the fuck is wrong with my legs?"

KaPrice turned her back so Dory couldn't see the tears that had formed in her eyes. At that moment, she was thankful for Big Gun being there because there was no way she could have given Dory the bad news. "Um, I think I need to step out for a minute," she stated and left.

Big Gun nodded his head at her letting her know that he understood. He waited for KaPrice to walk out and then told his friend the bad news. "Dory, man, the bullet hit you in the spine and it's gonna be a minute before you can use the lower part of your body again."

"Man, suck my muthafucking dick. Get outta here with that bullshit you talking. My legs work just fine!" He shouted and then tried once again to get out of the bed.

When he couldn't move his lower body, he became angry and asked, "How the hell I'm posed to function, dawg? I need my legs. And what about my dick. Nigga, how I'm supposed to live like this? Whoever did this shit to me should've just killed my ass because I ain't no more fuckin good. Fuck, they shoulda just killed me man."

"Dory, I know this shit is hard to accept but the doctor said that with some therapy you could get full use of your lower body back. It's just gonna take some time, man."

"Some time. The fuck I'm supposed to do until then? The fuck is gonna want a broke down ass nigga? Some time? Fuck these muthafuckas. They ain't the ones that can't walk. The fuck, man?"

"Come on, D. I'm gonna be with you every step of the way and Trap should be back in town any day now. We ain't gonna never leave your side. We got you, D. You ain't alone in this."

"I preciate you, Gun, but the last thing I want is a nigga helping me piss and shit. The fuck you gonna do, wipe my ass for me."

"No, but I am," KaPrice said as soon as she walked back in the room. "You got all us, Dory. Gun and Trap can help you with the heavy things and I, I'll help you with everything personal. I'll be there to help you in the tub and all. I ain't going nowhere."

Dory smiled at the comment KaPrice had made and although, he didn't fully remember her, he was glad that he had her. He looked deep in her eyes, and it gave him the feeling that she knew something. He figured he'd keep her around until he got more information and then he'd eliminate her.

***

"Damn, you two bitches ain't playin' with a nigga. That shit feels so damn good," Trap Town cried out while Kiara and Bree topped him off. He had tried to get them to put on a show with each other, but they acted like sucking pussy was beneath them. However, as long as things continued the way they were, he wouldn't push for anything else.

He listened to the women moan and held his head back. He knew that he was about to bust for the third time, and he was ready. "Yeah ladies. Here it comes. Go on and catch that shit for a nigga."

Trap Town rotated his hips and a few minutes later, he filled both their mouths up.

"Mmm, your shit is sweet," Bree said seductively. "I'm used to a nigga tasting like salt but this shit tastes like expensive candy."

"Bitch, you is stupid," Kiara said and got up off the bed. "Hey, I'm having a great time but I gotta get my ass outta here."

"Yeah, you damn sure don't want Malachi's dumb ass to come looking for you," Bree said with a smile.

Kiara didn't respond to her comment, instead, she went in the bathroom and shut the door behind her. She wanted to get her a final hit before she had to face Malachi.

Trap Town was recovering from the nut he had just bust when his cell vibrated. He picked it up and looked to see who the caller was and when he saw Big Gun's name on the screen, he quickly answered.

"What up yo?"

"Damn nigga, when you ass getting back in town? We got a situation."

"Gun, a nigga been in town all day, but I ran into Kiara and another bitch and them hoes been making my black ass shoot all day. Man, you should come join me."

"Nah, I'm good but ya boy Dory ain't."

"The fuck you mean?" Trap Town asked and sat up on the side of the bed. Bree walked over to him and started stroking his manhood, but he pushed her hand away when Gun told him the news. "Who the hell did it G? We got to get that muthafucka."

"We will when we find out who it was, but in the meantime we just gonna have to put in extra work." Big Gun had no intentions of telling Trap who had robbed and shot Dory. That was information he planned on taking to his grave.

"Aye man. Tell D I'm on my way. I'll see you when I get there," Trap said and hung up. He got off the bed and started getting dressed when Bree asked, "So, how we suppose to get home? You taking us?"

"Nah," he replied and pulled a wad of cash out his pocket. "Y'all split that shit. I gotta go." He walked out and left the two women behind.

Bree picked up the wad of cash and was going to put all of it in her purse, but she believed in karma so instead she counted it and split it down the middle. She knocked on the bathroom door to get Kiara's attention. "Yo Kiara, that nigga threw some bread on the bed and dipped on our ass. You want me to call us a taxi?"

Kiara opened the door and exhaled the smoke she held in.

"Bitch, don't be blowing that shit on me. I ain't no drugee," Bree said and fanned the smoke in the other direction. Kiara walked out of the bathroom and sat on the edge of the bed.

"I ain't no drugee either. I just like how it makes me feel. It keeps me from thinking about other shit," Kiara stated truthfully.

"Well, look I'm gonna get out of here. You coming with me?"

"I think I'm gonna chill and finish smoking the rest of my shit and then I'll call a ride. I had fun though. Maybe we can do this again some time."

"Yeah, I'm game. Just give me a call when you ready," Bree said and walked out, leaving Kiara behind. She pulled out her cell to call a cab, but a voice came from behind her and said, "You can call back and cancel that cab because you coming with me."

"Malachi, what are you doing here?" She asked in a nervous voice.

"Funny, I should be asking you the same thing. I'm here on business. What's your excuse?

Before Bree had a chance to answer, the motel room door behind her opened and Kiara stepped out.

***

"Give me the gun, Tasha. We gotta get rid of it," Kendrick said to his little sister.

Tasha didn't hesitate and handed him what he asked for. Kendrick then threw the gun over the bridge they crossed, and it landed in the water with a loud splash. He could see that Tasha was terrified but he would take a charge and go to prison before he would let his pride and joy go.

"Kenny, where are we going?" Tasha asked.

"We going to meet up with Cardo. He posed to be giving me a startup pack and me and Dre gonna make some bread. I want you to meet him, so he'll know you cool. It'll be less attention on a female than on us."

"You sure it's a good idea to get a girl involved Kenny? I think we should do it by ourselves. Besides, I got that other package I told you about. I don't' know if she should hang because girls talk too much."

"I 'ont run my mouth so you can save that speech," Tasha said with an attitude.

"Yeah, that's what all girls say but as soon as they get scared, they tell everything they know," Dre replied.

"What do you know anyway? You're just a kid jit trying to do big man things. You don't know nothing."

"Hey, y'all chill. Damn, can a nigga get a peace of mind," Kendrick said, and they stopped and sat on a log that was on the side of the trail.

"Man, what we stop for? Let's go get this stuff and get to work," Dre said.

Kendrick pulled a baggie out of his pocket and took out one of the rolled cigarettes that it contained. He put it to his mouth and lit the end and inhaled. When he exhaled and broke out into a fit of coughing Dre asked, "What kind of cigarette is you smoking to make you choke like that?"

Kendrick held his hand out so that he could pass the roll up and said, "Here, try some of this. It'll make you grow chest hair."

"I ain't trying to get no chest hair. I'm only seventeen and besides, that shit is nasty."

Tasha cut in and said flirtatiously, "Go head and smoke some, I heard it makes your dick bigger."

"Shoot my shit already like an anaconda. It's gonna be too big for my boxers if that's true."

Tasha and Kendrick laughed at his comment and watched as Dre took a hit of the joint. They laughed even harder when he choked on the smoke.

A sense of euphoria came over Dre immediately and he felt like he was walking in the clouds. He said, "Man I can feel my shit growing right now."

, "Let me feel it and see if you telling the truth." She reached her hand out, but Dre pushed it away and said, "Nah, only one woman can touch this snake and it damn sure ain't you."

Kendrick got up from the stump and said, "Man, y'all come on. Let's go make this run so we can take some shit over."

The trio started down the path on their mission. They were ready to come up and show the hood how shit was really done but they never could have imagined the obstacles they would face on the way to the top.

***

Valentine was more than ready to get settled into his new place. He still couldn't believe that he had come back. He felt like he could still feel Trey's presence and it hurt his heart as if the murder happened yesterday. He had already called and decided to have a legal visit with Daymion Myers. They had so much to talk about. He only hoped that Day wasn't too mad at him for leaving town so suddenly.

Daymion was just a kid back then but now he was a grown man who had been sitting in a cell for the last seventeen years of his life.

"Where are your credentials and what inmate are you here to see, sir?" The guard at the front gate asked when Valentine approached him.

"Justin Valentine, Attorney at Law and I'm here to see Daymion Myers," he showed the guard his credentials and photo identification. The guard checked everything out and then let him pass through where another guard would lead him to the attorney client visiting room.

Valentine felt queasy as soon as the door to the room shut. He looked around at the room which was empty except for a large brown table and four chairs. He wondered how many promises had been made inside the very room he stood in. He noticed the two-way mirror and wondered if their conversation would be listened to. He would ask the guard as soon as he returned with Daymion.

"Myers, you got a legal visit. Move your ass," the guard hollered.

Daymion has just got finished smoking a joint with Branch and Mellow and didn't like being fucked with. He just wanted to go back to his cell and relax. He didn't have any unfinished legal business, so he wondered what the visit was about.

"Man, Kiara better not be about to start no bullshit about my fucking son," he said out loud.

He had always feared that she would try to take his parental rights and if that's what the visit was about then whoever was there to see him could kiss his black ass. One more year and Dre would be eighteen and could make his own choices and Daymion couldn't wait.

He walked to the quad door and pushed the button to let the guard know he was ready and when the door opened, he was led down the hall to the other end of the prison where legal visits took place. His nerves were shot because not only was he high, but he was afraid he was about to lose his grip on Dre forever.

When they got to the door of the visiting room, the guard opened it and the man inside asked, "Aye man, is this session going to be recorded because I need privacy with my client?"

The guard replied, "No, sir. We only record when requested by law enforcement. You have complete privacy, Mr. Valentine."

"The fuck," Daymion said at the sound of the man's name. When the guard was gone Daymion asked, "Where the hell did you come from man and what the fuck you want from me?"

"Daymion, look I know I left town quickly when Trey was murdered but I couldn't handle staying here. That shit took a lot out of me man and I had to run. I'm sorry."

"You damn right you are. Nigga I needed you and you just up and ran like a fucking coward. You ain't even try to avenge Trey's death and now you show your ass back up here over twenty five years later. Well guess what? I don't want to hear what you gotta say because your word don't mean shit."

"Come on, Day, give me a chance, man. I know I fucked up. I made a promise to Trey that I'd take care of you but when I looked at you, I saw him. ManThat was my best fucking friend and staying here would have been the death of me. I had to leave. I couldn't take care of you when I couldn't even take care of my damn self. I had to go do something different, Day. Something to take my mind off of what I saw done to your brother."

"Yeah, well did it work? Was you able to move on and forget it all, including me?"

"Nah Day, that shit ain't work at all. When I lie in my bed at night, I can still see him. I can still see the blood and no matter what I do, it won't go away. I never forgot you though, I just had to get me right first."

Daymion tried hard not to cry while they talked about Trey, but he could honestly understand Valentine's pain because he still too felt that same pain. "I'm sorry, Val. I just. I ain't been the same ever since. I know you mean well man and I understand. I'm glad you came back."

The two men shared a brotherly hug and shed tears that they had been holding in. It felt good to release all the pain that they held inside.

Valentine asked, "I see you done got yourself in a bind. When you coming outta here?"

"Yeah, I got hemmed up with a bitch named Kiara. Bitch was only fifteen but had a body of a fucking grown ass woman. My dick made a choice that fucked me up for life. But I'm outta here soon. Matter of fact, I'm under three months now and I can't fucking wait."

"Heard you got a son. What's his name?"

"His name's Dreighton but I only got to meet him twice. The first time was when he came out and then again, a few months ago. Kiara ain't let him in my life because I ain't want shit to do with her. Her friend Kayla ended up bringing him at his request. Man, that lil nigga look just like my ass too."

"Damn, poor kid," Valentine said and shared a laugh with Daymion.

The two kicked it for a little longer and then Valentine finally said, "Aye, I'm here now and I give you my word, Day. I ain't leaving you again. I don't want the block to know I'm back yet. They ain't ready for my wrath, so keep that shit to yourself. I'm a go find out about your boy and when you get outta here, we got a lot of catching up to do."

"Thanks Val but Dre's all I care about. That bitch ain't doing right by him and I don't want to lose him to the streets like I did my brother."

"You won't lose him. I promise I won't let that happen."

The two parted ways but knew that they would meet again soon. Valentine would be back to see Daymion again but he would bring him news that he wouldn't want to hear.

Epilogue

One Months Later

"Hey, I'll see you when I get out there. Hold that shit down for me yo," Daymion said and hugged Branch goodbye.

Branch replied, "You know I got you as soon as you bounce. You keep it G in here, aight."

"Aight man. Be safe."

Branch walked out of the cell the two shared for the last time. He had done his time and was ready to be free. He had shit to do and pussy to fuck and couldn't wait.

The guard walked him down the corridor to the control room where he was identified to ensure he was the correct inmate leaving. Once all the paperwork was signed, he was then led outside and down a long fenced in sidewalk. He saw the black Escalade sitting at the end of the sidewalk and it made his dick hard. He couldn't wait to see his brother or the bitch he'd brought to service him on his first day out. He had gotten tired of jacking his dick and couldn't wait to put it in something wet.

When the end of the sidewalk came, the guard called on his radio for the gate to be popped open and when it did, he held his hand out and shook Branch's and said, "Good luck out there. I don't wanna see your face again."

"Bet that. See ya," Branch said and walked out into freedom.

He walked to the Escalade and opened the back door. He smiled when he saw a naked red bitch sitting in the back seat. Her nipples were hard and as soon as he got in and closed the door, he leaned over and pulled one into his mouth.

"Mmm, you did good by me bro. I can't wait to get up in this."

"Welcome home. I figured you'd want to dive right in, so I made sure she was ready."

"Well, you guessed right," Branch replied and unzipped his jeans. He pulled his hardened manhood out and said to the female, "Come on over here and put this in your mouth. Do me good, been a long time for a nigga."

The female was hesitant at first but when she turned her head, she caught the eyes of the driver looking at her through the rearview mirror. She finally got close to Branch and pulled him into her mouth. She sucked him like her life depended on it.

"So, are we set for when homie makes it out?" The driver asked.

"Yeah bro, nigga gonna come straight to us," Branch said and then moaned in pleasure.

"Mmm shit, bitch you can sure suck a dick." He then looked up in the front at his brother and asked, "Aye bro, what's this bitch name?"

The driver answered, "Kiara. That bitch's name is Kiara."

Lock Down Publications and Ca$h Presents
Assisted Publishing Packages

BASIC PACKAGE	UPGRADED PACKAGE
$499	$800
Editing	Typing
Cover Design	Editing
Formatting	Cover Design
	Formatting
ADVANCE PACKAGE	**LDP SUPREME PACKAGE**
$1,200	$1,500
Typing	Typing
Editing	Editing
Cover Design	Cover Design
Formatting	Formatting
Copyright registration	Copyright registration
Proofreading	Proofreading
Upload book to Amazon	Set up Amazon account
	Upload book to Amazon
	Advertise on LDP, Amazon and Facebook Page

***Other services available upon request.
Additional charges may apply

Lock Down Publications
P.O. Box 944
Stockbridge, GA 30281-9998
Phone: 470 303-9761

Submission Guideline

Submit the first three chapters of your completed manuscript to ldpsubmissions@gmail.com. In the subject line add **Your Book's Title**. The manuscript must be in a Word Doc file and sent as an attachment. Document should be in Times New Roman, double spaced, and in size 12 font. Also, provide your synopsis and full contact information. If sending multiple submissions, they must each be in a separate email.

Have a story but no way to send it electronically? You can still submit to LDP/Ca$h Presents. Send in the first three chapters, written or typed, of your completed manuscript to:

LDP: Submissions Dept
P.O. Box 944
Stockbridge, GA 30281-9998

DO NOT send original manuscript. Must be a duplicate. Provide your synopsis and a cover letter containing your full contact information.

Thanks for considering LDP and Ca$h Presents.

NEW RELEASES

BLOODLINE OF A SAVAGE **BY PRINCE A. TAUHID**

THE MURDER QUEENS 4 **BY MICHAEL GALLON**

THE BUTTERFLY MAFIA **BY FUMIYA PAYNE**

KING KILLA 2 **BY VINCENT "VITTO" HOLLOWAY**

BABY, I'M WINTERTIME COLD 3 **BY MEESHA**

THESE VICIOUS STREETS **BY PRINCE A. TAUHID**

TIL DEATH 2 **BY ARYANNA**

CITY OF SMOKE 2 **BY MOLOTTI**

STEPPERS **BY KING RIO**

THE LANE **BY KEN-KEN SPENCE**

MONEY GAME 2 **BY SMOOVE DOLLA**

THE BLACK DIAMOND CARTEL **BY SAYNOMORE**

CRIME BOSS 2 **BY PLAYA RAY**

THUG OF SPADES **BY COREY ROBINSON**

LOVE IN THE TRENCHES 2 **BY COREY ROBINSON**

TIL DEATH 3 **BY ARYANNA**

THE BIRTH OF A GANGSTER 4 **BY DELMONT PLAYER**

PRODUCT OF THE STREETS **BY DEMOND "MONEY" ANDERSON**

Coming Soon from Lock Down Publications/Ca$h Presents

BLOOD OF A BOSS VI
SHADOWS OF THE GAME II
TRAP BASTARD II
By **Askari**

LOYAL TO THE GAME IV
By **T.J. & Jelissa**

TRUE SAVAGE VIII
MIDNIGHT CARTEL IV
DOPE BOY MAGIC IV
CITY OF KINGZ III
NIGHTMARE ON SILENT AVE II
THE PLUG OF LIL MEXICO II
CLASSIC CITY II
By **Chris Green**

BLAST FOR ME III
A SAVAGE DOPEBOY III
CUTTHROAT MAFIA III
DUFFLE BAG CARTEL VII
HEARTLESS GOON VI
By **Ghost**

A HUSTLER'S DECEIT III
KILL ZONE II
BAE BELONGS TO ME III
TIL DEATH II
By **Aryanna**

KING OF THE TRAP III
By **T.J. Edwards**

GORILLAZ IN THE BAY V
3X KRAZY III
STRAIGHT BEAST MODE III
By **De'Kari**

KINGPIN KILLAZ IV
STREET KINGS III
PAID IN BLOOD III
CARTEL KILLAZ IV
DOPE GODS III
By **Hood Rich**

SINS OF A HUSTLA II
By **ASAD**

YAYO V
BRED IN THE GAME 2
By **S. Allen**

THE STREETS WILL TALK II
By **Yolanda Moore**

SON OF A DOPE FIEND III
HEAVEN GOT A GHETTO III
SKI MASK MONEY III
By **Renta**

LOYALTY AIN'T PROMISED III
By **Keith Williams**

QUIET MONEY IV
EXTENDED CLIP III
THUG LIFE IV
By **Trai'Quan**

THUG OF SPADES | COREY ROBINSON

I'M NOTHING WITHOUT HIS LOVE II
SINS OF A THUG II
TO THE THUG I LOVED BEFORE II
IN A HUSTLER I TRUST II
By **Monet Dragun**

THE STREETS MADE ME IV
By **Larry D. Wright**

IF YOU CROSS ME ONCE III
ANGEL V
By **Anthony Fields**

THE STREETS WILL NEVER CLOSE IV
By **K'ajji**

HARD AND RUTHLESS III
KILLA KOUNTY IV
By **Khufu**

MONEY GAME III
By **Smoove Dolla**

MURDA WAS THE CASE III
Elijah R. Freeman

AN UNFORESEEN LOVE IV
BABY, I'M WINTERTIME COLD III
By **Meesha**

QUEEN OF THE ZOO III
By **Black Migo**

CONFESSIONS OF A JACKBOY III
By **Nicholas Lock**

THUG OF SPADES | COREY ROBINSON

JACK BOYS VS DOPE BOYS IV
A GANGSTA'S QUR'AN V
COKE GIRLZ II
COKE BOYS II
LIFE OF A SAVAGE V
CHI'RAQ GANGSTAS V
SOSA GANG III
BRONX SAVAGES II
BODYMORE KINGPINS II
By **Romell Tukes**

KING KILLA II
By **Vincent "Vitto" Holloway**

BETRAYAL OF A THUG III
By **Fre$h**

THE MURDER QUEENS III
By **Michael Gallon**

THE BIRTH OF A GANGSTER III
By **Delmont Player**

TREAL LOVE II
By **Le'Monica Jackson**

FOR THE LOVE OF BLOOD III
By **Jamel Mitchell**
RAN OFF ON DA PLUG II
By **Paper Boi Rari**

HOOD CONSIGLIERE III
By **Keese**

183

PRETTY GIRLS DO NASTY THINGS II
By **Nicole Goosby**

PROTÉGÉ OF A LEGEND III
LOVE IN THE TRENCHES II
By **Corey Robinson**

IT'S JUST ME AND YOU II
By **Ah'Million**

FOREVER GANGSTA III
By **Adrian Dulan**

GORILLAZ IN THE TRENCHES II
By **SayNoMore**

THE COCAINE PRINCESS VIII
By **King Rio**

CRIME BOSS II
By **Playa Ray**

LOYALTY IS EVERYTHING III
By **Molotti**

HERE TODAY GONE TOMORROW II
By **Fly Rock**

REAL G'S MOVE IN SILENCE II
By **Von Diesel**

GRIMEY WAYS IV
By **Ray Vinci**

Available Now

RESTRAINING ORDER I & II
By **CA$H & Coffee**

LOVE KNOWS NO BOUNDARIES I II & III
By **Coffee**

RAISED AS A GOON I, II, III & IV
BRED BY THE SLUMS I, II, III
BLAST FOR ME I & II
ROTTEN TO THE CORE I II III
A BRONX TALE I, II, III
DUFFLE BAG CARTEL I II III IV V VI
HEARTLESS GOON I II III IV V
A SAVAGE DOPEBOY I II
DRUG LORDS I II III
CUTTHROAT MAFIA I II
KING OF THE TRENCHES
By **Ghost**

LAY IT DOWN I & II
LAST OF A DYING BREED I II
BLOOD STAINS OF A SHOTTA I & II III
By **Jamaica**

LOYAL TO THE GAME I II III
LIFE OF SIN I, II III
By **TJ & Jelissa**

IF LOVING HIM IS WRONG…I & II
LOVE ME EVEN WHEN IT HURTS I II III
By **Jelissa**

BLOODY COMMAS I & II
SKI MASK CARTEL I, II & III
KING OF NEW YORK I II, III IV V
RISE TO POWER I II III
COKE KINGS I II III IV V
BORN HEARTLESS I II III IV
KING OF THE TRAP I II
By **T.J. Edwards**

WHEN THE STREETS CLAP BACK I & II III
THE HEART OF A SAVAGE I II III IV
MONEY MAFIA I II
LOYAL TO THE SOIL I II III
By **Jibril Williams**

A DISTINGUISHED THUG STOLE MY HEART I II &
III
LOVE SHOULDN'T HURT I II III IV
RENEGADE BOYS I II III IV
PAID IN KARMA I II III
SAVAGE STORMS I II III
AN UNFORESEEN LOVE I II III
BABY, I'M WINTERTIME COLD I II
By **Meesha**

A GANGSTER'S CODE I &, II III
A GANGSTER'S SYN I II III
THE SAVAGE LIFE I II III
CHAINED TO THE STREETS I II III
BLOOD ON THE MONEY I II III
A GANGSTA'S PAIN I II III
By **J-Blunt**

PUSH IT TO THE LIMIT
By **Bre' Hayes**

THUG OF SPADES | COREY ROBINSON

BLOOD OF A BOSS I, II, III, IV, V
SHADOWS OF THE GAME
TRAP BASTARD
By **Askari**

THE STREETS BLEED MURDER I, II & III
THE HEART OF A GANGSTA I II& III
By **Jerry Jackson**

CUM FOR ME I II III IV V VI VII VIII
An **LDP Erotica Collaboration**

BRIDE OF A HUSTLA I II & II
THE FETTI GIRLS I, II& III
CORRUPTED BY A GANGSTA I, II III, IV
BLINDED BY HIS LOVE
THE PRICE YOU PAY FOR LOVE I, II ,III
DOPE GIRL MAGIC I II III
By **Destiny Skai**

WHEN A GOOD GIRL GOES BAD
By **Adrienne**

TRUE SAVAGE I II III IV V VI VII
DOPE BOY MAGIC I, II, III
MIDNIGHT CARTEL I II III
CITY OF KINGZ I II
NIGHTMARE ON SILENT AVE
THE PLUG OF LIL MEXICO II
CLASSIC CITY
By **Chris Green**

THE COST OF LOYALTY I II III
By Kweli

A GANGSTER'S REVENGE I II III & IV
THE BOSS MAN'S DAUGHTERS I II III IV V
A SAVAGE LOVE I & II
BAE BELONGS TO ME I II
A HUSTLER'S DECEIT I, II, III
WHAT BAD BITCHES DO I, II, III
SOUL OF A MONSTER I II III
KILL ZONE
A DOPE BOY'S QUEEN I II III
TIL DEATH
By **Aryanna**

A KINGPIN'S AMBITION
A KINGPIN'S AMBITION **II**
I MURDER FOR THE DOUGH
By **Ambitious**

A DOPEBOY'S PRAYER
By **Eddie "Wolf" Lee**

THE KING CARTEL I, II & III
By **Frank Gresham**

THESE NIGGAS AIN'T LOYAL I, II & III
By **Nikki Tee**

GANGSTA SHYT I II &III
By **CATO**

THE ULTIMATE BETRAYAL
By **Phoenix**

BOSS'N UP I, II & III
By **Royal Nicole**

THUG OF SPADES | COREY ROBINSON

I LOVE YOU TO DEATH
By **Destiny J**

I RIDE FOR MY HITTA
I STILL RIDE FOR MY HITTA
By **Misty Holt**

LOVE & CHASIN' PAPER
By **Qay Crockett**

TO DIE IN VAIN
SINS OF A HUSTLA
By **ASAD**

BROOKLYN HUSTLAZ
By **Boogsy Morina**

BROOKLYN ON LOCK I & II
By **Sonovia**

GANGSTA CITY
By **Teddy Duke**

A DRUG KING AND HIS DIAMOND I & II III
A DOPEMAN'S RICHES
HER MAN, MINE'S TOO I, II
CASH MONEY HO'S
THE WIFEY I USED TO BE I II
PRETTY GIRLS DO NASTY THINGS
By Nicole Goosby

STEADY MOBBN' I, II, III
THE STREETS STAINED MY SOUL I II III
By **Marcellus Allen**

189

LIPSTICK KILLAH I, II, III
CRIME OF PASSION I II & III
FRIEND OR FOE I II III
By **Mimi**

TRAPHOUSE KING I II & III
KINGPIN KILLAZ I II III
STREET KINGS I II
PAID IN BLOOD I II
CARTEL KILLAZ I II III
DOPE GODS I II
By **Hood Rich**

STEADY MOBBN' I, II, III
THE STREETS STAINED MY SOUL I II III
By **Marcellus Allen**

WHO SHOT YA I, II, III
SON OF A DOPE FIEND I II
HEAVEN GOT A GHETTO I II
SKI MASK MONEY I II
By **Renta**

GORILLAZ IN THE BAY I II III IV
TEARS OF A GANGSTA I II
3X KRAZY I II
STRAIGHT BEAST MODE I II
By **DE'KARI**

TRIGGADALE I II III
MURDA WAS THE CASE I II
By **Elijah R. Freeman**

THE STREETS ARE CALLING
By **Duquie Wilson**

THUG OF SPADES | COREY ROBINSON

SLAUGHTER GANG I II III
RUTHLESS HEART I II III
By **Willie Slaughter**

GOD BLESS THE TRAPPERS I, II, III
THESE SCANDALOUS STREETS I, II, III
FEAR MY GANGSTA I, II, III IV, V
THESE STREETS DON'T LOVE NOBODY I, II
BURY ME A G I, II, III, IV, V
A GANGSTA'S EMPIRE I, II, III, IV
THE DOPEMAN'S BODYGAURD I II
THE REALEST KILLAZ I II III
THE LAST OF THE OGS I II III
By **Tranay Adams**

MARRIED TO A BOSS I II III
By **Destiny Skai & Chris Green**

KINGZ OF THE GAME I II III IV V VI VII
CRIME BOSS
By **Playa Ray**

FUK SHYT
By **Blakk Diamond**

DON'T F#CK WITH MY HEART I II
By **Linnea**

ADDICTED TO THE DRAMA I II III
IN THE ARM OF HIS BOSS II
By **Jamila**

LOYALTY AIN'T PROMISED I II
By **Keith Williams**

THUG OF SPADES | COREY ROBINSON

YAYO I II III IV
A SHOOTER'S AMBITION I II
BRED IN THE GAME
By **S. Allen**

TRAP GOD I II III
RICH $AVAGE I II III
MONEY IN THE GRAVE I II III
By **Martell Troublesome Bolden**

FOREVER GANGSTA I II
GLOCKS ON SATIN SHEETS I II
By **Adrian Dulan**

TOE TAGZ I II III IV
LEVELS TO THIS SHYT I II
IT'S JUST ME AND YOU
By **Ah'Million**

KINGPIN DREAMS I II III
RAN OFF ON DA PLUG
By **Paper Boi Rari**

CONFESSIONS OF A GANGSTA I II III IV
CONFESSIONS OF A JACKBOY I II
By **Nicholas Lock**

I'M NOTHING WITHOUT HIS LOVE
SINS OF A THUG
TO THE THUG I LOVED BEFORE
A GANGSTA SAVED XMAS
IN A HUSTLER I TRUST
By **Monet Dragun**

THE STREETS MADE ME I II III
By **Larry D. Wright**

QUIET MONEY I II III
THUG LIFE I II III
EXTENDED CLIP I II
A GANGSTA'S PARADISE
By **Trai'Quan**

CAUGHT UP IN THE LIFE I II III
THE STREETS NEVER LET GO I II III
By **Robert Baptiste**

NEW TO THE GAME I II III
MONEY, MURDER & MEMORIES I II III
By **Malik D. Rice**

CREAM I II III
THE STREETS WILL TALK
By **Yolanda Moore**

LIFE OF A SAVAGE I II III IV
A GANGSTA'S QUR'AN I II III IV
MURDA SEASON I II III
GANGLAND CARTEL I II III
CHI'RAQ GANGSTAS I II III IV
KILLERS ON ELM STREET I II III
JACK BOYZ N DA BRONX I II III
A DOPEBOY'S DREAM I II III
JACK BOYS VS DOPE BOYS I II III
COKE GIRLZ
COKE BOYS
SOSA GANG I II
BRONX SAVAGES
BODYMORE KINGPINS
By **Romell Tukes**

THUG OF SPADES | COREY ROBINSON

CONCRETE KILLA I II III
VICIOUS LOYALTY I II III
By **Kingpen**

THE ULTIMATE SACRIFICE I, II, III, IV, V, VI
KHADIFI
IF YOU CROSS ME ONCE I II
ANGEL I II III IV
IN THE BLINK OF AN EYE
By **Anthony Fields**

THE LIFE OF A HOOD STAR
By **Ca$h & Rashia Wilson**

THE STREETS WILL NEVER CLOSE I II III
By **K'ajji**

NIGHTMARES OF A HUSTLA I II III
By **King Dream**

HARD AND RUTHLESS I II
MOB TOWN 251
THE BILLIONAIRE BENTLEYS I II III
REAL G'S MOVE IN SILENCE
By **Von Diesel**

GHOST MOB
By **Stilloan Robinson**

MOB TIES I II III IV V VI
SOUL OF A HUSTLER, HEART OF A KILLER I II
GORILLAZ IN THE TRENCHES
By **SayNoMore**

KILLA KOUNTY I II III IV
By Khufu

BODYMORE MURDERLAND I II III
THE BIRTH OF A GANGSTER I II
By **Delmont Player**

FOR THE LOVE OF A BOSS
By **C. D. Blue**

MOBBED UP I II III IV
THE BRICK MAN I II III IV V
THE COCAINE PRINCESS I II III IV V VI VII
By **King Rio**

MONEY GAME I II
By **Smoove Dolla**

A GANGSTA'S KARMA I II III
By **FLAME**

KING OF THE TRENCHES I II III
By **GHOST & TRANAY ADAMS**

QUEEN OF THE ZOO I II
By **Black Migo**

GRIMEY WAYS I II III
By **Ray Vinci**

XMAS WITH AN ATL SHOOTER
By **Ca$h & Destiny Skai**

PROTÉGÉ OF A LEGEND I II
LOVE IN THE TRENCHES
By **Corey Robinson**

KING KILLA
By **Vincent "Vitto" Holloway**

BETRAYAL OF A THUG I II
By **Fre$h**

THE MURDER QUEENS I II
By **Michael Gallon**

TREAL LOVE
By **Le'Monica Jackson**

FOR THE LOVE OF BLOOD I II
By **Jamel Mitchell**

HOOD CONSIGLIERE I II
By **Keese**

BORN IN THE GRAVE I II III
By **Self Made Tay**

MOAN IN MY MOUTH
By **XTASY**

TORN BETWEEN A GANGSTER AND A
GENTLEMAN
By **J-BLUNT & Miss Kim**

LOYALTY IS EVERYTHING I II
By **Molotti**

HERE TODAY GONE TOMORROW
By **Fly Rock**

PILLOW PRINCESS
By **S. Hawkins**

SANCTIFIED AND HORNY
by **XTASY**

THE PLUG OF LIL MEXICO 2
by **CHRIS GREEN**

THE BLACK DIAMOND CARTEL
by **SAYNOMORE**

THE BIRTH OF A GANGSTER 3
by **DELMONT PLAYER**

BOOKS BY LDP'S CEO, CA$H

TRUST IN NO MAN
TRUST IN NO MAN 2
TRUST IN NO MAN 3
BONDED BY BLOOD
SHORTY GOT A THUG
THUGS CRY
THUGS CRY 2
THUGS CRY 3
TRUST NO BITCH
TRUST NO BITCH 2
TRUST NO BITCH 3
TIL MY CASKET DROPS
RESTRAINING ORDER
RESTRAINING ORDER 2
IN LOVE WITH A CONVICT
LIFE OF A HOOD STAR
XMAS WITH AN ATL SHOOTER

www.ingramcontent.com/pod-product-compliance
Lightning Source LLC
Chambersburg PA
CBHW070509260626
47161CB00004B/1504